Critical acclaim for
The Man who Wanted to I

'Augustine said that man was evil, Pelagius that man was neutral. This meant that man did not need God's grace and could attain heaven through his own efforts alone. This, if we regard heaven as a secular notion signifying a sempiternal state of social happiness is the philosophy of the Danish state as presented in Stangerup's nightmare. The nightmare is the more terrifying because it is very close to a known waking situation — one in which society has decreed that man must not suffer either physically or spiritually, that the state has the duty of securing minimal health and prosperity for all, and that concepts like guilt and anxiety have no meaning. Søren Kirkegaard, the greatest of Danish thinkers, has no place in this innocent polity.

The fact of human aggression is admitted, but this is taken care of by the control of the media which must exhibit nothing of an antisocial nature. Even Hans Christian Andersen is purged of his grosser elements, and television is as arid as the earth, lifeless as the waters. Pelagius has defeated Augustine. There is room neither for *mea culpa* nor exculpation. Crime is merely social maladjustment.

The beneficent engineering of the Scandinavian state is well under way, the engine oiled, its tenders efficient and amiable. Unlike the visions of future horrors we love to read because the true future, we know, cannot possibly contain them, the near-actuality of Stangerup's book chills more than anything I have read in years. We do not have to fear a Big Brother named out of a brutally realistic irony but a genuinely loving one in rolltop sweater and jeans, his image multiplied as by a Xerox machine.'

Anthony Burgess, Inquiry

The Man who Wanted
to be Guilty

HENRIK STANGERUP

The Man who Wanted to be Guilty

a novel

Translated into English by
David Gress-Wright

Marion Boyars
London · New York

First published in paperback in Great Britain and the United States
in 1991 by Marion Boyars Publishers
24 Lacy Road, London SW15 1NL
26 East 33rd Street, New York, NY 10016

Distributed in the United States and Canada by
Rizzoli International Publications, New York

Distributed in Australia by
Wild and Woolley, Glebe, NSW

Originally published in hardcover in 1982 by Marion Boyars Publishers
© This version Henrik Stangerup 1982, 1991

An earlier version of this book was first published in Denmark
under the title *Manden der ville vaere skyldig*
by Gyldendal Paperbacks.

British Library Cataloguing in Publication Data

Stangerup, Henrik
The man who wanted to be guilty.
1. Danish fiction — Translations into English
2. English fiction — Translations into Danish
1. Title   II. Manden der ville vaere
skyldig. *English*
839.8'1374[F]   PT8176.29T3

ISBN 0–7145–2930–3 Paperback

Library of Congress Catalog Card Number 81–52332

Cover photo by permission of Pathe-Nordisk Film Distribution.

Printed in Great Britain by Southampton Book Company.

"Guilt — what might that be? Is it sorcery?
Do we not know precisely how a man becomes guilty?
Will no one answer? Is it not a matter of the
utmost importance for all those present?

My mind stops — or rather, am I losing it?
One moment I am tired and lethargic, almost dead
from lack of interest; the next I am raging,
dashing desperately from one end of the world to
the other to find someone upon whom to vent my rage.
The entire content of my being is screaming at odds
with itself. How did I become guilty? Or am I not
guilty? Why, then, am I called so in all tongues
of the world? What sort of miserable invention is
human speech, if it says one thing and signifies
something else?"

Søren Kierkegaard

CHAPTER ONE

They had been at the AC meeting most of the evening and were quite tired. Attending the AC meetings (Aggression Control) was optional, but pressure from the other people in the superblock had gradually brought them to the point of taking part, not so much out of a fear of being isolated, as out of a fear of what might happen to Jasper in school and in the leisure center. In order to endure the meetings they had, accordingly, adopted a special technique which consisted in taking an exaggerated part in the various exercises and the subsequent self-analysis as though it were all a game that hardly had any personal significance. Edith, paradoxically enough, was best at the physical exercises. She was able to hammer away at a rag doll for half an hour and lie on the floor kicking a foam-rubber monster until it came completely apart. He, on the other hand, was better at the defamatory exercises. There was no limit to his ability to discover obscene expressions when he had to berate and insult an indeterminable and almost faceless man who was shown to him in the form of a rapidly changing series of slides. He put a lot of effort into finding a new swear word for each frame, and had achieved eighty per cent coverage. Their only problem was the subsequent self-analysis in the presence of the Helpers until they agreed that their 'remarkable' and 'unpredictable' aggression must be due to an unhappy childhood in each case, combined with malevolent influences. Had they been left alone by their parents? God yes, more than that! For days! Had they read too many of those comics subsequently banned by the government? Yeah, nothing but! Batman! Superman! Rip Kirby!

Nevertheless a growing feeling that lately Edith had begun to see a purpose in the AC meetings was bothering him and becoming a source of irritation. Her ironic distance to it all was disappearing. She was no longer excited by all the tales about their horrible childhood which they succeeded in putting over on the Helpers. Were they beginning to get to her? Had she blown their tactics to the Helpers? He thought back: didn't the Helper seem suspicious this evening when he had made up that story about how his father used to lock him in the coal cellar when, as a boy, he refused to finish his meals? He looked at Edith. She was lying on the sofa she had upholstered with the new fashion material she had found in *Home and Person* and cleaning polish off her nails. She put the bits of lacquer in a little pile on the glass coffee table next to the Japanese bonsai tree. She had trimmed it with nail-scissors and razor blades over the last ten years they had lived in the superblock, so that now it looked like a real tree – *was* a real tree, eight inches high and four wide. The fashion for Japanese bonsai trees had really got big when all the trees in the city died from seeping road-salt. It was only in the suburbs, out here, with all those super-blocks, that a few trees still lived. In fact one of them grew right outside their windows and miraculously bloomed every year. He got up, taken with a sudden urge to see whether the tree had any buds. As he edged by between Edith and the coffee table he thought of waving his hand over the pieces of lacquer making them flutter out over the edge of the table and onto the rug so that Edith would have to crawl around on all fours picking them up. But he controlled himself and reached the window: it was too dark to see anything but an outline of the tree – of course, he could have told himself that. The lights had gone out in most of the apartments opposite.

He knew that he would not be able to sleep if he went to bed now. Edith yawned and finally stopped her picking. He went to the kitchen and got out the ice-tray.

'Are you going to drink again?' she said from the living-room.

He didn't answer.

'Torben, dammit, I asked you a question!'

What sort of an irritated tone of voice was that? Why the interrogation all of a sudden? He didn't feel like replying and knocked out the ice-cubes with a spoon under the hot water faucet. He drank what he pleased, when he pleased. Nevertheless he felt embarrassed and awful enough to fill the glass with whiskey and immediately take three great gulps so that she wouldn't complain of his lack of moderation. He put water and ice into the remainder and went into the living-room, where Edith was busily collecting the pieces of lacquer in a sheet of paper.

'I know why you didn't answer,' she said. 'You really think that I *personally* mind your drinking!'

'Well, if not, then why the third-degree?' he asked and deliberately swirled the ice-cubes in the glass.

'For your own sake,' she said. 'You know you have kidney trouble!'

'As far as I know, it's the *liver* that's harmed by alcohol. Kidneys, that's pills, and I haven't taken any for months.'

'So you say.'

Yes, so I say, he considered answering, but why go on letting the snowball roll. Edith was grouchy, and it was her right to be that way once in a while. She had gone back to the sofa and pulled her legs up under her. Now that there was no more polish to pick off her nails she began cutting them. Didn't she think of anything but nails? He became annoyed with her again and tried to hold it in check, but now that he thought about it, it wasn't just tonight that she was grouchy. She had been grouchy the day before and the day before that, she had been grouchy for weeks. For months? When had they last been to bed together? Two months ago? Three? He knew what would happen shortly, when they went to the bedroom. He

9

would lie down first. Then she would get under the covers, smelling of soap, wearing the sexless nightgown he suspected she wore on purpose to keep him off. He would pat her cheek and hope that she might be a little bit willing, but she would rapidly go to sleep, and after lying for an hour or so staring at the ceiling the moment would come when he would have to release his erotic fantasies by taking the matter into his own hands, but quietly, oh so quietly, so she wouldn't wake up and ask him *if he was doing that again*. Another hour would elapse before he fell asleep, usually just before feeling the vibrations in the mattress which told him that it now was her turn to get satisfaction, whatever she was dreaming about. Why? Why must it be like that? What invisible barrier had slowly risen between them during the last ... couple of *years* perhaps?

'I'm bored!' he said all of a sudden in a way that ought to tell her that if she wanted fun, he certainly wouldn't mind.

'Bored, how?' she asked.

That was precisely the answer he was hoping she wouldn't give. But he refused to give up so soon:

'By everything. Everything bores me, the apartment, the superblock, the view with the stupid tree which has probably already rotted from the roots.'

He was about to go on: '... and your nail-picking.' But instead he added:

'And especially by those stupid AC exercises! God how I hate them!'

'They're not that silly.'

'What are you saying?'

'You have to admit that there's some sense to them.' She said.

He could feel the hairs rising on his neck and arms. Even the lump in his throat made its appearance as he realized that they had gained control of her. He gave up trying to figure out when Edith had given way; the most important thing was that she had. The tactic they had adopted to cheat the Helpers had proved useless. He saw a connection between her surrender and their lack of sex for these past months. And he saw more than that, he suddenly saw the rest of both their lives circumscribed by definite lines, lines that were the same as those affecting their neighbors. Lines which cut out hopes and dreams that somewhere there was a place that they would reach one day: some distant corner of the world with a chance of a better life. Perhaps a life in poverty or without unnecessary material comforts and insurances from head to toe, but a life of freedom with green trees and fresh air and rivers which were not poisoned, a life of daily challenges without the boredom that insinuated itself like a chronic buzz into one's eardrums. From now on however it would be the superblock day in and day out, and if they became bored with the superblock, it would be another superblock in another supertown. From now on it would be AC meetings, final dissolution in senseless work in an office which gave him migraine on account of its unbalanced ion count, "educational" tv after work, leafing through *Home and Person*, sleepless nights without the least sign of love, and – what excitement! – Sunday competitions among the inhabitants of the superblock for the prettiest bonsai trees. And at the end of it all: a pension, forced transfer to the world's most modern, most sanitary and most boring old people's home with direct access to the crematorium. He could see it now: at some point, in a few years, maybe even in six months or so, he too would lose his power of resistance. He would admit to an "egocentric world-view", an "antisocial escape psychosis", an "ego-tripping mentality", or any one of the other Helper expressions for whatever was socially unacceptable. He would surrender his dreams and thereby lose the last remains of his aggressive sense of humor, then one fine day – and this, to him, was the worst of it all – he would really come to believe that it was the height of happiness and bliss if Edith won a prize for her bonsai.

He turned on the tv even though he knew perfectly well that the program – the twelfth and final all-night discussion of children and literature – would make him see red. A female lecturer in the social sciences was leading eight participants in the discussion, and evidently there was some technical problem, because she was continuously glancing nervously about the studio. Then suddenly her face filled the screen. She smiled apologetically, pushed her glasses back over her hair and began addressing the viewers with some opening remarks. She said that many people probably would be offended by the pro and con discussion scheduled for tonight – a discussion about Hans Christian Andersen himself. But why not discuss Hans Christian Andersen? Just because he was Hans Christian Andersen? Weren't many of his tales antisocial in their celebration of the loner, of the defiant genius? Did not Hans Christian Andersen in his autobiography, however sensitive and well-written it was, reveal a singular lack of understanding of other people, of the social whole? Did he not consider his poor upbringing merely as a stepping-stone to personal advancement? And as far as his stories went, one might well say that there were certain things in them which were not in the least different from the productions of the brothers Grimm which – thanks to the great efforts of a team of psychologists – were now purged of their demons so that children would not wake up in the middle of the night bathed in perspiration. She would not venture to say whether it was now Hans Christian Andersen's turn – she was merely the moderator – but anyway, that was the subject for discussion. Was Hans Christian Andersen, the unimpeachable, the divine treasure of the nation, to be kept as he was or was it time for revision in view of future editions?

'*The Snow Queen*,' she said, 'yes, let's begin with *The Snow Queen*.'

'Listen to her! How prejudiced she is!' he snarled.

He turned off the tv. He had met that sociologist at parties a couple of times, and each time he had wondered how she had ever managed to make a career of it: her ignorance was matched only by her coy, smug self-confidence. Now she had enraged him just enough to allow him a couple of hours of fighting with Edith. Only by way of a deliberately provoked clash would he be able to tell how bad things really were with her:

12

'But you like her, maybe? Perhaps you even think she's *right*?'

'Well, maybe she is,' she replied.

'How maybe?'

'Well, if it's true . . . that it's harmful for Jasper to read his . . . stories.'

'How harmful?' he said, pursuing her.

Her voice became shrill:

'I don't know!'

She had begun to doubt. He wanted to get at that doubt.

'Harmful, *how*, I asked!'

She felt for a cigarette, lit it and inhaled three times in a row. He couldn't keep her eyes on him. Her glance strayed about the room, and once or twice she threw her head back, girlishly, to give the impression that she wasn't bothered at all. Then she got up and stood with her back to him:

'You know, bad dreams at night . . . and like that'

She turned around and looked straight at him, and now her eyes held fear. She backed off three paces:

'What *is* it, Torben? Tell me what it is! Why do you look at me like that? Torben, right now you hate me! Admit it, you *hate* me!'

He recalled the time the great child-raising debate rolled across the country and excited the population as never before or since. The government had proposed two pieces of legislation which were closely related. Firstly a general ban on children's books and comics which contained the least intimation of violence, a cult of the loner or of the sort of adventure which emphasized distant, exotic places over the familiar and the workaday. Secondly, and in relation to this, the much more radical proposals of compulsory tests for everyone wishing to have children: tests in elementary developmental psychology, practical tests of social interaction and child contact, and – supervised by social workers, psychologists and doctors – tests on the mental and physical condition of the applicants. Only by passing these tests with an above-average grade could one obtain the right to a 'child certificate' (those who were parents

13

already would automatically receive one). However, the authorities would at any time have the power to take back the child certificate from a couple and have their children raised by the state or by mentally sound foster parents.

These two proposals had almost become law when the population suddenly rebelled, and protest marches and strikes paralyzed the nation for months. Popular anger culminated in a mass march on the government palace, led by Edith and himself among others, and at one point Edith had jumped on a speaker's box and had delivered an ardent and impromptu speech, which had been broadcast live on television. For some reason it became the decisive event; at any rate, the government announced the following day that it would withdraw the proposals. But a year later they were carefully brought forward again, and on this occasion they were passed without much protest, thanks to months of active and insidious manipulation of the public via the press and television: the proposals were put in the interests of the children. Didn't people want to see happy and secure children? Didn't everyone want a future population of socialized and harmonious people, free from the troublesome thoughts which dangerous reading and an upbringing by mentally unstable parents would inevitably engender? Finally it was claimed that at most a tenth of one per cent of the population would fail the tests. The tenth of a per cent, however, quickly became one per cent, and that became ten and later twenty, and was now hovering around twenty-five. Those who had no difficulty in obtaining the child certificate were the intellectuals; curiously enough, the one group with the most mentally unstable people, the highest divorce and suicide rate, and the greatest consumption of alcohol, drugs and medication. This group had no trouble in getting the certificate for one very cogent reason: the intellectuals were traditionally the group from which new ideas came, and the best way to neutralize them was to give them the certificate along with the ever-present fear that it could be taken from them.

He had no doubt that this was how things were when he

looked at Edith standing before him, nervously biting her nails. The thought of the Edith who some years ago had jumped up and delivered a speech which caught not only him and the others in the protest march by surprise, but evidently also the government and its staff of social workers and sociologists who had prepared the proposals. What frightened her now was the threat that, if they did not submit to the system, they would one day receive the first warning in the shape of a grey slip saying that they perhaps were not ideal as child-raisers. Later they would receive the blue slip and finally the much-feared red slip which meant that Jasper would be taken from them and put somewhere where they would never find him. He knew that right now Edith had one hope – he could read it in her eyes, in the way her hands began shaking – that he would calm down, whatever the cost: calm down a little bit more every day and finally accept the rules of the game as she had done for a long time – apparently, before he had noticed.

He approached her, he wanted to take hold of her shoulders, kiss her and hug her, stroke her and caress her, be tender and rough at the same time. But she kept avoiding him; she was really frightened, he could see that. That made him even angrier, and suddenly, without him realizing it, she began running around the room, and him after her, jumping over chairs, overturning the table and violently throwing the empty whiskey tumbler into the kitchen where it crashed against the dishwasher. Finally he got hold of her. She was like a limp rag, a heap of jelly: she collapsed on the floor without resistance as though she expected him to beat her, something he had never even dreamt of doing before, but which he now wanted to do because she was almost begging him to. Her nails were piercing the skin of his thighs just below his crotch. At that moment, instead of beating her, he wanted to make love to her. He wanted to turn her over on the floor, tear her clothes off and make love to her so fiercely that she would become

15

herself again and lose her fear. Then they could lie on the floor afterwards and light the classic cigarette and talk as they had in the old days about the possibilities of another and better life: without Helpers, without child certificates, without super-blocks, without boredom. They could dream again of a life which would inspire him to start his writing again and inspire her to see new meaning in her job as a film editor because the films she would be cutting would be full of imagination and joy.

But he couldn't. He could not make love to her. He realized, in a flash of insight, that Edith had made the right choice in resigning herself to the inevitable. Sensing that his despera-tion was leading nowhere, that tomorrow would be like today and yesterday made him unable to love her. His desperation took hold like a dull pain behind his eyes as he sat down on the edge of an upturned easy chair and stared at Edith who was still lying crouched on the floor and clenching her hands in the rug. The world consisted of the four walls around him, a dying tree for a view, housing blocks one after the other with thousands of people, preparing themselves for sleepless nights full of inflamed erotic fantasies, the sound of the wind making an iron gate slam shut, the boom of a supersonic jet making all the window panes vibrate and beyond that – nothing. Yes, Jasper of course, Jasper in his room dreaming. About what? What did children dream of nowadays? About nothing? Muddy colors without contrast smeared into each other? Indistinct, blurred vistas of iron and concrete, with no sun, no shadow and no creatures of the imagination, neither the slimy and terrible ones like dragons nor the warm, round, friendly and furry ones?

He went into the kitchen, sat down on the floor and this time drank straight from the bottle as though it were beer. He had once read that one could die from drinking alcohol like that, but he didn't care. When he had drunk half the bottle he had the feeling that Edith had appeared in the doorway. It was only when she cleared her throat repeatedly that he looked up at her and deliberately put the bottle to his lips and drank the rest. She must have pulled herself together in the bathroom very quietly because all of a sudden she was again the apathetic, nail-clipping Edith she had been earlier in the evening, with coolly judging eyes and no hint that she had just been through a serious crisis. Her hands were no longer shaking and she had even made time to remove the smears in her make-up. He couldn't help laughing hysterically when he began seeing her double, and shortly after three times.

'You ought to see yourself!' he said.

'What do you mean?' she asked sternly, as though she was copying his way of asking.

He pointed at the doorway:

'Your face is there ... and there ... and there ...!'

He heard what she answered. But he had to finish laughing before he could concentrate to make sure that he had really heard right.

'Don't you think I should summon the Helpers?' she had said.

'Repeat that!' he shouted, and stopped laughing. 'Just repeat what you said!'

He got up. Fell over. Got up again.

'Now I'm calling the Helpers,' she said, and left the doorway.

He staggered after her but failed to stop her pressing the button in the hallway.

'Now I've done it,' she said.

'But how about Jasper?' he stammered. 'When they see me like this ...'

'There is such a thing as a child certificate for divorced mothers,' she said in a hard voice.

For the first time in his life he realized what it was like to hit a woman. First he just hit her weakly, but then fury took hold. He struck harder and harder, at her solar plexus, her face, her sides. He couldn't stop, and when she began shouting for help he took her head and battered it against the wall. When she sank lifeless to the floor he took her head again and hammered it against the tile floor. He was no longer in control of himself; he was overcome by rage and felt that his eyes were bursting from his head. The blood vessels in his temples throbbed and expanded and for a moment it was as though his own head was being hammered against the floor. He didn't stop, even when she began bleeding at the mouth.

Then he heard voices from behind. Shortly afterwards the front door was unlocked and two Helpers fell on him and lifted him up by the arms. At that moment he vomited.

CHAPTER TWO

He couldn't understand why they were so friendly. The nurses were friendly to him, in the state hospital refectory they were friendly, the guards were friendly and the psychiatrists were friendly – especially the one who took care of him and who had a conversation with him once a week which usually lasted most of the afternoon. The psychiatrist was a short, jowly man with small, curious eyes behind intellectual spectacles. Every time he went to see him (in his private home which was on the outskirts of the hospital zone) a bottle of sherry was ready and waiting. The conversations took place in the psychiatrist's study which was covered from floor to ceiling with books, including many novels and anthologies of poetry. The psychiatrist was well-known outside his own circle for his books and articles on literature; an interest which occasionally led his colleagues to object that he ought to keep to professional journals. The psychiatrist's attraction to fiction was probably one of the reasons why he had been put under his care: among the novels in his collection there were also the two he had written in the early seventies, both in their original editions. During a conversation, after the first few weeks of desperation when he had realized that in a moment of alcoholic frenzy he had beaten Edith to death, the psychiatrist had amused himself by analyzing his male characters professionally. He in turn, had amused himself by replying that here they were in the classic situation where a psychiatrist solemnly, and using a rigid conceptual apparatus, was, through analysis, reaching universal conclusions and hypotheses that were clearly expressed in the text, but only in artistic fashion and hence bursting all limits. Did the psychiatrist believe that it was something new to him that his characters were depressive, that they passionately sought experience and not theory, that their feelings were blocked, that they were egocentric, idiosyncratic and oppressed by maternal fixations and escapism?

'Perhaps that is why I always seek out literature and not specialist theories, something which irritates my colleagues,' the psychiatrist politely replied. 'What you said about "bursting all limits" ... But tell me, why did you stop writing, anyway?'

'Why ... why ...,' he said. 'I don't suppose there is any one good reason.'

Nevertheless the psychiatrist had succeeded in eliciting from him a reply which began with the Creation of the World.

He had written both novels in the south of France where he and Edith had gone to clear matters up for themselves after the youth rebellion of the sixties in which they had taken part right up to the occupation of the universities and the establishment of liberated territories across the country. They had been on soft drugs, had lived in hippie camps and had even been in a Scandinavian student brigade in Cuba to help with the sugar harvest. But as the spirit of the sixties evaporated, what had begun as enthusiasm ended in sectarianism, depression and paranoia. New crowds of young people kept appearing, claiming that they alone stood for true revolution, and this was no longer a revolution that consisted of taking off one's pants and throwing flowers at the police; instead it was Molotov cocktails and potatoes bristling with razor blades. It was the time for general extermination of the pigs, and the pigs were everywhere; the pigs were the cops and the politicians and the businessmen, but the pigs were also invisible, to be sure, they could disguise themselves as friendly, cooperative university professors, as flower children and as friendly artists who dreamed of their childhood. The paranoia became worse week by week, and everybody became afraid of the other. The daily fear of being passed on the left ensconced itself as a permanent growl in his stomach, and he and Edith got to the point where they could not walk the street and see a meter maid without snarling 'Fascist!'. Months of self-destructive hair-splitting and hateful discussions followed in various Copenhagen communes. At the university, where he still pretended to study literature when he wasn't writing the (ever more cryptic) stories he occasionally published, the old and formerly all-powerful professors were carried out with nervous break-downs or fled to Australia, only to be replaced by a team of newly-hatched inquisitors who with ideological perfectionism quivering at the corners of their mouths set out to dump most of world literature in the trashcan of history. No dialogue was possible any longer, and at this point the decision to run away from it all ripened in him – away from a city which was becoming more and more morbid and vicious, not just psycho-logically, but even physically. But his paranoia was so deep that it was only after a while that he dared confide in Edith – he feared the worst: being considered a renegade in his wife's eyes. It turned out, however, that she felt as bad as he did and that she also hadn't dared admit it. And she was even able to tell him that she was pregnant.

'The old story,' smiled the psychiatrist. 'Go on!'

He described the night they crossed Town Hall Square after deciding to sell all they owned to travel south and settle down there, their happiness, their sense of being reborn. For a while they had abandoned the nightmare of mankind perfected and once again sensed what it meant to be free.

Within a week they were in a small village twelve miles from Nice and he had started writing the novel about the university lecturer who gets squeezed between the old professors and the students, gives up on his dissertation (how old-fashioned) and ends up in the state hospital believing quietly and happily that

21

he is the reincarnation of Dag Hammarskjöld. The book wrote itself, so to speak, chapter after chapter being torn from the typewriter. He knew all of it so well, had felt the novel coming for the last couple of years. And at the same time Jasper was growing in Edith's belly, and they were surrounded by fragrant herbs and flowers, and at the nearby cafe he met daily with communist workers and peasants who were just like communists were supposed to be: friendly, un-neurotic, un-puritanical and possessed of an elementary belief that human worth was not something that had to be discovered by way of mental self-laceration, insane discussions, nervous breakdowns and Nordic-pietist resentment and suspicion.

They returned to Denmark when Edith was six months pregnant and he had finished the novel. It was the middle of the summer, the restaurants in Tivoli were full of beer and sandwiches and an important publisher opened his doors to him. The novel was immediately accepted and was published just as Edith was giving birth. The favorable reviews and good sales enabled all three of them to return to the village: now he wanted to write a novel about a commercial journalist who suddenly hears the message from the underground and who changes his life from one day to the next, gives up his wife, his house, his car and his whiskey for an addict, a rented room with a mattress, a chain around his neck and Marx under his pillow, but who of course winds up being misunderstood and burns himself alive. But the novel was too much like the first one; he got stalled in chapter two – until he chanced on the notion of having himself talk about himself in every other chapter, relentlessly and honestly: young author flees Copenhagen to the sunny south, where he tries to save his political conscience by writing madly about his other self who wants desperately to be young with the young and who winds up setting fire to himself. Back again to Copenhagen with the manuscript, immediate acceptance, once more favorable reviews on the day it appeared (*'Finally: an artist among the rebels'*), booksellers' prize, four printings, book club, paperback, tv programs, translations ...

'But you know all that,' he said.

'Go on, go on,' the psychiatrist answered.

Yes, what more could he say? Was there more to tell? They remained in Denmark; now they had enough money and bought a large old house in fashionable Frederiksberg. For several months there was hardly a mass-media discussion in which he wasn't involved. He felt enormously energetic and managed to distance himself sufficiently from the extremists who became more and more aggressive and despérate as they began having children and were faced with the obligations of life. For a while he hovered above the waters with remarks such as: 'I am hoping for a society which will blend John Ford and Karl Marx.' But gradually exhaustion and nerves came back, and meanwhile he and Edith were living far beyond their means. Increasingly it was being said that he was repeating himself and rapidly approaching the point when he would no longer be able to renew himself, and that he would most likely wind up as a sour, old-fashioned book reviewer for what remained of the conservative cultural élite. Desperation began creeping up on him again. The south of France became a fragrant memory of happiness and humanity. Bills and warnings from the central tax register came tumbling through the letter-box, a collection of articles and polemics was badly received, he behaved in a childish and egocentric fashion at several cultural seminars to which he was invited, and he began drinking. At the same time it was as though society at large was moving imperceptibly away from what had been the dreams of democracy.

'But you know that as well,' he said tiredly.

'I would like to hear *your* version,' the psychiatrist answered.

He tried to collect his impressions from the last ten to fifteen years. He knew that his account was not just, that it was based on highly subjective evaluations, and was closely tied to his personal defeat. And of course developments were not purely bad: much of what they had fought for in the sixties had become reality. Women's rights had been assured, worker

23

participation in the factories was a reality, and heavy industry had come under the control of what some people called the state, others the people – as had insurance companies and banks. But at the same time it was as though every step in the right direction entailed a number of steps in wrong directions. What use was the vote for eighteen- and later sixteen-year-olds if nobody bothered to vote in elections any more? The sense of impotence grew in the population and boredom competed with conformism in the concrete blocks which seemed to have taken over half Denmark. Who ran what and how? Nobody knew. The jails were closed one after the other, but was this a socialist state? Was it capitalist? Nobody discussed ideology any more. The situation was a new one, but nobody had found a name for it. Alienation might be a name for it, if one wanted to use an expression from the sixties, but it was something far vaguer, far less definable, far deeper and more massive. And there was nowhere to put the responsibility. Politicians apologized and apologized on tv, but their apologies could not remove the bond of almost feudal obligations consisting of ever-rising taxes and ever-rising rents in ever more badly built tenements and superblocks. Nobody had a cent, but on the other hand everybody had large numbers of wage cards, credit cards and payment orders for more and more obligatory insurance in a world where there were fewer and fewer hidden dangers and the average life-span was perpetually increasing. Billions were used to combat pollution, but it was already too late to save the Baltic, more and more superhighways were built, more and more of nature was destroyed. Drug and tranquillizer abuse rose rapidly, and the suicide rate began to look really sinister. And then all the patent solutions – everybody had patent solutions for everything, not least in the Sunday color supplements, where the 'in people' in their refurbished farmhouses dispensed advice to the population in the concrete blocks: grow herbs on your balcony! Make a corner of your living room into a jungle! Grow bonsai trees!

What was wrong? Nobody could say. Did not the state have

only one aim: The Common Good from Cradle to Grave? But why was nobody happy then? What was happiness? Nobody could say – least of all the thousands of sociologists and psychologists who had completed their studies in the seventies and who, because they failed to revolutionize society as they had dreamed of doing when they occupied the universities, compensated through reforms which entailed the abolition of all education favoring individualism, prohibition of 'dangerous' television and 'dangerous' children's literature and generally everything glorifying the exotic and the heroic. In their place there were 'voluntary' AC exercises and an explosion of courses in group dynamics, the stopping of all support of art and research which was not immediately socially oriented, and much else of the same kind – including the law of forced tests for all who wanted children as the crowning insult. Incessantly new laws for the Common Good were passed, and new theories of how people could best be fitted into social reality were debated. As migrant workers from poorer countries took over the more boring work (without the rights and the influence which their Danish comrades enjoyed) Denmark had become a nation of two groups: those who worked in the tax sector, the import sector, the export sector, the agricultural sector, the insurance sector and all the other sectors – and those who worked in the therapeutic sector. In between was the tiny group of people like himself – old rebels without official credentials, writers, journalists, directors without producers, tv people, actors and drug addicts. When their finances finally collapsed they had to sell the villa in Frederiksberg and move into a superblock, and he had to take a part-time job in BLIMP – the Bureau of Language Improvement. But there was no money to spare and hence no chance of travelling even for a fortnight or so a year – his demoralizing work, which was impoverishing the language, just enabled him to keep the payment orders at arm's length.

Why indeed had he stopped creating? What could inspire him? Concrete and bonsai trees? What human crises could he describe and what breakthroughs could be made in a universal and disturbing way, when the Helpers were telling the people daily that limits were necessary, that the tangible was more important than the universal and that human crises must be considered and treated rationally and in a way which did not disturb?

Why had he wound up where he was? He didn't really need a psychiatrist to diagnose his situation, he concluded, and utter desperation gripped him again. What use was his talking like this – there was no way he could recall Edith from the dead. He buried his face in his hands as though that would succeed in freeing him from his vision of them hammering her head against the wall and the hard floor.

'The mice that can't escape . . .' said the psychiatrist.

'What do you mean?' he asked taking his hands away from his face.

'I was just thinking of a famous experiment of some years ago. A mouse colony was allowed to develop in limited space, but under the best possible conditions, unlimited food, no diseases, no natural enemies. After a while the group lost the ability to carry out anything but the most elementary survival functions. The mice began attacking one another, mothers abandoned their young and much more of that sort . . . because there was no longer any possibility of self-defence and . . . escape.'

'What you are saying . . .'

'Nothing that you should take for granted. But sometimes I wonder if there isn't more to be said for the similarity of men and mice – animals generally – than is commonly admitted. It has been heretical for quite some time now to claim that man, apart from being a symbol-making social being is also a species – an animal with animal needs.'

Certainly a philosopher, and maybe a poet had been lost in this psychiatrist, he thought and was relieved that the conversation was taking a more general turn. The psychiatrist removed his glasses and polished them, and suddenly he lost the authority of his position; he seemed mole-like and alone behind his desk and among his innumerable books.

26

'Would you like another glass?' he asked.

'Yes please. But what happened to the mice at the end?'

'I can't really remember, and as I said, don't take the comparison for more than it's worth – man is not an animal, after all.'

Gradually the talks with the psychiatrist became lengthy philosophical discussions. He no longer felt like a patient with a doctor. They were equals, finding a common pleasure in talking philosophy, ethics, society and last but not least the future awaiting mankind. Would it be even less freedom, even more control, even *less* room – or an unexpected liberation in many areas, not least the spiritual? They sketched out a theory that their age was sort of a quiet before the storm. There were no more adventures, no new horizons to reach for, no experiences either on the inner or on the outer plane – in short: no way of escape. Man had made himself lord of all and had been hit by an immense ennui which rendered him unable to defend himself against oppression. But what might seem to be the end of history – spiritual drought and the destruction of the imagination, might in fact be the beginning of a new, amazing epoch. They themselves might not experience anything other than the feeble beginnings of this epoch, but the more they let their imaginations roam the less they doubted that it had to come. Soon mankind would move into space for good – not just an astronaut here and an astronaut there – but by the thousands, by the millions. Men would reach new suns, new galaxies, become a part of the cosmos, of a logical and mystical whole of encompassing beauty. New paths of knowledge would abolish the old, the linear, the down-to-earth. Art, ethics and religion would again coalesce, but without the pedantic rules of behavior which had crippled the soul for centuries. The end of the twentieth century would soon be regarded as an unimportant interlude, a few grey and sad decades with no other function than to serve as a link between the first period of human development that ran from antiquity to the first Moon landings and the ultimate state of man's cosmic liberation. He made the psychiatrist admit that perhaps society right now was, after all, rather like the mouse colony. Only those with imagination would realize that this limited space was not the whole world but only a tiny point in the infinite where man's destiny was fated to be fulfilled.

These wide-ranging talks (now and then they smiled shyly at one another when they felt they had ventured rather too far) gave him back his courage. Desperation and remorse for what he had done still sat deeply in him, and he would regularly awake screaming – a nurse would come running – because he saw Edith's bloody face before his eyes. Nevertheless he found a new balance – and he began working. The talks with the psychiatrist called on his need to write – novels, stories, essays, whatever.

He calculated that, following his conviction, he would probably need to remain at the hospital for a couple of years at least, and he intended to use the time to write down his visions of a future without any oppression, where the eye would meet beauty and human life would be lengthened by decades, perhaps even centuries, on new green planets where the seas were not polluted and animals did not die of mercury and DDT poisoning. He wanted to write it all down, not least for Jasper's sake. When he got out, perhaps he could get the chance to have him back if he kept on pestering the authorities. If nothing else, he would discover where Jasper was. And then he would secretly initiate him into the world that awaited him and which he was to help create. Jasper was to be brought up to be an adventurer, a revolutionary, a scientist and an artist, all at the same time – to know that human history had barely begun and that hope had always won out during times when repression was at its worst.

His day was carefully regulated, and he calmed down more and more – not least thanks to the pills they gave him whenever depression set in. He had been moved into a room of his own which he was allowed to decorate as he wished by hanging pictures on the walls (he still dared not put a photo-

28

graph of Edith on the windowsill). He was allowed the rug which he had kept since his student years, a globe of the world with a light in it, a typewriter, paper and some books. After breakfast, which he took together with the other patients in one of the innumerable refectories, he went for a long walk in the hospital park nodding to the various passers-by, doctors, nurses and, not least, patients. Some of the patients paid him no attention but walked with their eyes fixed on the ground: they were probably under medication, he thought. Others were excessively friendly and seemed to enjoy the park quite as much as he. Before too long he wanted to explore it thoroughly, especially the part where the deeply insane were kept who were allowed to behave just as they wanted – they had their own theater for those who thought they were actors, studios for those who wanted to paint and sculpt, ceramic workshops, a parliament for those who dreamed of being politicians, a small publishing house with duplicators and much else of that kind. That part of the hospital was popularly known as Happiness Park and was, as an experiment, famous throughout the world. Here there was a miniature society which had nothing to do with a hospital in the usual sense – the patients even had their own apartments. He had not, however, heard of anyone becoming well enough in Happiness Park to be able to return to normal society.

After lunch he visited the local municipal library. As the weeks went by he received a permit to go out for two hours every afternoon. But where would he go? Ride the underground? Go to a dismal cafeteria where a murderous neon light illuminated nothing? Take a walk among the superblocks of the neighborhood and count dying trees? No, he preferred the library. He had even succeeded in persuading a librarian in the reading-room to let him have some of the science fiction novels the library hid away in the basement so that children wouldn't stumble across them. He quickly skimmed through Orwell, Huxley and Bradbury, but that wasn't really the orientation he was looking for. It was easy enough to view the future pessimistically, he thought and smiled because he knew that 1984 was only chronologically in the future. He enjoyed the lesser-known authors far more, those who imagined how exciting it all would be.

When he got back from the library he drank tea in the canteen. Then he sat down at the table in his room and started to make notes and drafts. He set himself the goal of writing, during the years at the hospital, two, perhaps three novels, and he hoped that they would all appear simultaneously. He felt the joy of writing again, the joy of inventing people, describing the galaxies and the colonization of hitherto uninhabited worlds. Then he thought of Edith who loved him the most when he sat bent over his desk, lost in writing. But the joy became pain: he recalled the south of France in the early seventies. The fragrance of lavenders. Edith's swelling belly. Her laughter ringing through the small cafes. He rang for a pill, and when he had taken it, he worked calmly on.

One day he decided to take a close look at Happiness Park. When he got there he discovered that it was fenced in on all sides. He pressed his eye to a hole in the fence and saw a strange mixture of cabins, a theater, speaker's boxes and various buildings which he gathered held the publishing division, the parliament, the ceramic workshop and the apartments of the insane. Strange people in strange garments were walking around among all the buildings and seemed to be engaged in normal activities. A theatrical group was rehearsing not far from the fence; in another spot a poet in a cape was declaiming Byron; in a third place a painter had set up his easel. Then he suddenly heard a voice behind him:

'Best you don't come here!'

He turned around. It was the psychiatrist. Fortunately he was smiling:

'The Happiness Park experiment is still at its vulnerable, experimental stage, so we don't really want spies hanging around, if you will permit my saying so ...'

'I was simply unable to control my curiosity,' he said.

They walked towards the administration building.

'I'm going to an important meeting,' said the psychiatrist. 'But it was fortunate that I caught you ...'

The psychiatrist stopped, as though he wanted to hide something. Then he went on as before:

'The patients are allowed to live out their dreams completely. That, I guess, is the essential secret of Happiness Park. Naturally along with new medication which has appeared during the last few years and which helps to "open" them up, if I may say so.'

The psychiatrist seemed nervous. What was it he wouldn't tell? They came to the administration building. Now the psychiatrist became formal in a way he never had before:

'You're free,' he said.

'*Free*?' he asked.

'We've decided that you can return to society with no difficulty.'

He felt the earth give under him. A completely new kind of desperation rose up in him and made his heart beat far too violently. Something was wrong. Something was *very* wrong. When the psychiatrist kept on looking at him coldly and reflectively, he became afraid. Afraid of he knew not what.

'But you can't release me just like that!' he said and could hear how pitiful he sounded. 'I'm guilty! I committed a murder! I killed my wife!'

Was the psychiatrist retreating? Was he ashamed of something? And what was that something? No, the psychiatrist became even more testy:

'Guilt!' he said in a slightly contemptuous tone of voice. 'Don't you know that society is in the process of abolishing the concept of guilt once and for all!'

Society! The psychiatrist pronounced the word as though it were absolute, concrete, infallible, and divine. He could hardly comprehend that he was facing the same man with whom he had been discussing philosophy, ethics and man's future for weeks. What had happened to the lover of literature, the philosopher, the dreamer?

31

'But I killed her!' he heard himself repeat. 'I killed her!'

'Or you were driven to it. There *is* a difference.'

'Killing is killing!'

Now the psychiatrist became angry:

'An eye for an eye, a tooth for a tooth. Is *that* what you want?'

'No, no, of course not, for God's sake! But I'm still guilty of murder!'

'Take it as you please,' the psychiatrist said, giving up or at least, seeming to, and disappeared into the administration building.

He thought of what he was about to return to, and his eyes became moist. Then he told himself that it was ridiculous that a man his age should weep.

CHAPTER THREE

They had removed anything which might remind him of her;
her dresses, her underclothes, her shoes. The things in her
bedside table were gone. The blowup in the bedroom of him
carrying the proofs of his first novel and embracing a nine-
months-pregnant Edith had also been removed – only the
nail-holes in the wall were left. Even the little picture of him
alone (signed 'to the world's most lovely Edith') which she had
kept on the bedside table was gone. From the wardrobe in the
hall they had taken her coats, her rubber boots and her
umbrella. All photographs of her alone or with others had
been carefully removed from the albums they had kept from
the mid-sixties to the mid-seventies. In the bathroom only her
toothbrush was left; they must have been in doubt as to which
one was hers. On the other hand they had gone to great
trouble to remove the dressing table that she had inherited
from her grandmother and which they had spent an entire
morning hoisting up the front of the building and in through a
window. Perhaps it had been carried down the stairs as so
much firewood. They had really done a thorough job, he had
to admit. Whoever they were.

At first he thought that her family had been there, but they
would hardly have seen any purpose in removing the blowup,
the picture on her bedside table and the photographs in the

albums. A completely impassive plan had been followed, and no one could be behind it other than the Helpers in the super-block. Or perhaps somebody from a department specializing in removing such disturbing mementos. Suddenly he thought of Jasper. He hurried to his room. Here, also, everything had been removed, the bed, the electric train, the miniature race-track, the bowdlerized edition of Grimm's fairy tales, Jasper's teddy bear which he'd had since he was tiny, his clothes, his stuffed birds, his hamster – everything. Even the walls had been newly painted in the places where Jasper had liked to draw. He stood in the room for some minutes. Then he returned to the living-room.

The Helpers hadn't removed the bonsai tree, of course. It was still on the table and next to it was the pair of scissors which had helped to drive him crazy. He plunged them into the tree, carried it out to the hallway and dumped it into the garbage chute. Later he tried to sort out the innumerable payment orders which had piled up in the hallway while he had been gone, but he gave up after a while and felt more like letting them go the same way as the bonsai tree. What if he refused to pay and they came and removed the rest of the things in the apartment, now that he was no longer a respons-ible husband and father? He was alone, he could do what he wanted, quit his job at the bureau, get a small advance from his old publisher, write at night, sleep by day, bring home the girls he wanted. He made himself see the bright side of the situation but failed to suppress the feeling of hopelessness. Free, he thought – you're free. They all want the best for you, they understand that you weren't in control of yourself when you did it, society wants you to be a happy and harmonious person again. You've got all the chances, he thought – but he couldn't keep down his tears. You're your own master, he thought – and noticed how his hands were shaking.

The storm rattled the window-panes and he expected one of them to crack at any moment. Spring was still a long way off, it seemed, and the tree outside the living-room didn't seem to have any buds yet. He was smoking the twentieth cigarette since he had got back that morning and his fingers were yellow-stained from tip to base. He dared not look at himself in a mirror. He sensed that he had bloodshot eyes, that he had lost a lot of hair and at least twenty pounds at the hospital. He felt hungry and went to the kitchen, but there was only some dried-up liver paté and some stale smoked fish in the refrigerator. He started heating water for coffee but of course discovered at once that there was no coffee in the house. There was a bottle of tepid schnapps in an empty beer-crate. He sipped from it; it tasted awful. He kept drinking, however, until he could feel the effects in his blood-stream. It's just a matter of an ad in the paper he thought – then you'll have a housekeeper! Maybe you'll even be lucky enough to get one of the last of the good old-fashioned kind who know everything from pickling cucumbers to baking bread and ironing shirts. What did he have to complain about? That he didn't have to spend ten years in a medieval jail?

He took the elevator down and walked along the long subterranean corridors that connected the various parts of the superblock. On one occasion a lot of children came towards him, led by a teacher. When he got close he saw that it was Jasper's class from school and momentarily hope rose in him. A couple of the boys smiled at him as they passed by. Then one of them shouted:

'Is Jasper sick?'

The teacher took hold of the boy carefully but firmly, and soon the class had disappeared up a staircase. The last one to disappear was the teacher. She just barely turned around to look at him. Did her glance hold judgement? Or even worse: condescension, compassion, supercilious 'understanding' ...? Did she know what he had done? Did anyone around here know what he had done? Did they know it where he worked, did his friends know? Maybe there had been nothing at all about it in the papers.

In the superblock canteen nobody turned around to look at

him. No hasty glances, no whispering in corners. The wait-resses smiled at him as usual, and one of them recommended the special of the day: roast pork with hashed brown potatoes. 'Then you won't have to eat the cardboard chicken you hate so much!' she said and showed him to a place in the corner. He accepted her offer whilst attempting a smile, but he still felt like a shadow, a ghost. They must be able to tell from looking at him what he had done, just as they could always tell when as a boy he had lied either in school or to his father. 'You'll get red ears!' they said in school. 'You have a black mark on your forehead!' his father said, 'a big black mark right between the eyes!' He fumbled with the salt-cellar and leafed through a local advertisement paper lying next to him on the chair. Then he realized that without his noticing he had put two fingers between his eyes. Now you're being silly, he thought, and later he couldn't help looking to see if his fingers really were black: now you're really going crazy!

He tried to get a hold on himself. Of course nobody could see by his expression that he had killed Edith. And nobody would ever know. It was part of the procedure to keep it silent. He was not supposed to be open to harassment, neither here where he lived nor at work. He was supposed to get every chance to fill his place in society again. And if anyone asked where Edith and Jasper had gone, he was supposed to think of some story or other to the effect that they had been divorced and that Edith had gone to South America with a businessman and that they had decided that Jasper should go with her for some years to return later to attend Danish high school.

Nevertheless he felt that there was something missing. Why hadn't the psychiatrist prepared him by letting him know that he was only going to be in the hospital a few weeks? Why the friendliness and the openness first and then suddenly: here you are, you can go! What did it say in the journals that the psychiatrist had written, in the journals that the Helpers or the police had kept? That he was to be kept under observation constantly, but unobtrusively, so as not to upset him? Would they demand that he report to the Helpers where he was going when he left the superblock? Would they revoke his passport? And did he have any chance of getting the child certificate and therefore Jasper back? When the waitress brought the roast pork all these questions had stolen his appetite, and he could only chew furiously on the rubbery pieces of fried rind and drink a glass of sugary-sweet Portuguese wine. Then he put the money on the table, hurried out of the canteen and went to the offices where the Helpers were to be found. His heart was in his throat when he knocked, but he wouldn't give up, he wanted to know the exact reason why he had suddenly been set free, and with what right the Helpers had removed Edith's things. He had not yet heard of a law allowing them to steal from the population!

'Are you the one who's been rummaging around in my apartment?' he asked immediately after he had stepped inside and a Helper, not much over twenty-five years of age, had asked him to sit down in an easy-chair. The Helper wore jeans and a turtleneck sweater; the perpetual and classic uniform of the psychologist or social worker, or whatever he was. I wish he had the courage and the honesty to wear a professional white coat, he thought.

'Since you ask me so directly, you also deserve a direct answer,' said the Helper. 'And the answer is yes.'

'You *personally*?' he asked.

'It doesn't really matter whether it was I or somebody else,' the Helper answered and sat down on a table, letting his legs swing free in a relaxed manner.

'By what right?'

'Right? ... well now. Let's say we did it for your sake. It's often the everyday memories, the little things, that stop a person in your situation ... shall we say, stop him getting *on* ...'

He sensed that he was losing the desire to go on. He couldn't possibly penetrate the armour-plated shielding of relaxed affability. Suddenly the Helper took out a file from the desk drawer and began studying it.

'Is that my dossier?' he asked, feeling frightened.

The Helper nodded.

'What does it say about me?'

'Nothing that wouldn't do you credit,' the Helper said.

'Can I see it?'

'Listen,' the Helper said. 'Isn't it enough that you are free? That you can arrange your own life as you like?'

'Do you mean, that I can come and go as I like?'

Now he had shown the Helper his entire hand of cards.

'Why shouldn't you be able to do that?'

'I mean ... without letting you know where I'm going?'

The Helper looked at him condescendingly:

'Tell me, do you think we're planning to keep you under *observation*? You are your own master, I tell you.'

'I was just thinking ...'

'Nothing to think about. But if you should suddenly feel depressed and start blaming yourself ... just take one of these ...'

The Helper gave him a small bottle of red and green pills: 'But only one a day!'

Just as he was about to let himself into his apartment he realized that he had forgotten to shut the garbage chute. On a sudden impulse he threw the bottle of pills the same way as the bonsai tree and the pair of scissors. How could he know what was in those pills? Perhaps chemicals which would tranquillize him all day and deprive him of the inspiration to write. Was that what they wanted: that he should end up a brainless nodding doll? No, he wanted to live through his depression by his own strength of will and nothing was better suited to that than work. They weren't going to stop him writing novels, not even by shutting him out of a hospital where his days were organized. The novels were to become his personal comeback, but more than that, they would literally prepare mankind for the new, wonderful world which awaited it in the not too distant future.

As soon as he entered his apartment he began rearranging

the furniture. He rolled the tv set into Jasper's empty room so that he wouldn't be tempted to switch it on. The sofa adjacent to the living-room window he pushed against a wall, and in the middle of the room he put his desk. He wanted space around himself. Typewriter, paper, pens, his notes from the hospital – he put everything in careful order on the desk. After pulling the curtains shut and trying various ways of lighting the room he put some paper in the typewriter. 'Chapter one'.

He wrote no more that day. Suddenly he felt hungry, but it was at a time when the shops had already closed and he had no urge to visit the canteen once more. Instead he drank the rest of the schnapps and took a scalding hot bath. He dried himself with his back to the mirror because he still dared not look himself in the eyes. Then he went to bed. How long did he sleep? It was certainly dark outside when he suddenly leaped out of bed and began running around the apartment, turning on all the lights that he could find. He sat down at his desk, but when he saw the blank paper in the typewriter he got up again and sat down on the sofa. But even there he could not relax: the nightmare which had chased him out of bed kept on driving him through the apartment, turning on lights. He had dreamed of Edith. They were walking in Copenhagen. It was a lovely summer day, as summer days still were fifteen years ago. Edith was nine months pregnant, almost. There was Tivoli, friendly Copenhageners and tourists with their eight millimeter cameras, hot dog stands, beer and sidewalk cafes with parasols in all the colors of the rainbow. He had Edith by the arm. They were whistling some tune or other. He tickled her gently. She laughed. He kissed her and she fondled his neck. And then, suddenly, it happened. Just outside Tivoli everything went black in his head for a moment and without knowing why he began hitting her in the face, across the chest and finally in the stomach. None of the passers-by reacted, but kept smiling amiably, the hot dog men continued to dispense hot dogs, and under the parasols beer was still being served. Even when Edith fell to the sidewalk lifeless with blood streaming from her mouth no one reacted. Then he awoke and threw aside the covers, and now he was sitting in the apartment with all the lights on, one moment at his desk, the next on the sofa and finally on all fours in the kitchen trying to find something to satisfy his insane hunger.

When he finally fell asleep it was morning, and he had sat in vain in Jasper's empty, moonlit room trying to find a tv program from Germany or Sweden. He slept until late morning. Then he washed himself in the kitchen and drank four glasses of the chlorinated water to fill his stomach. He knew now quite clearly that he would never be able to work in that apartment because he would have nightmares every night. He had to settle abroad. But to do that he needed money. So, he had to visit his old publisher.

'Well, well, is it you?' said the publisher and showed him into the sanctum sanctorum. 'Long time no see!'

'Yeah, really!'

Suddenly he realized that he had forgotten to shave. It made him feel insecure.

'And Edith?' the publisher asked. 'She's fine, I hope?'

'Sweden,' he said, without knowing why he chose that country.

'Vacation?'

'We've ... separated ...'

'I'm sorry. Didn't mean to pry. Are you bringing me a new manuscript?'

'Not yet. Some day.'

'What about?'

'The future.'

'Oh no, no more future stories. Contemporary stories, Torben, present-day stories! But as a writer you never were very socially oriented ...'

What had happened to his publisher? In the old days he always was at a loss for words, spilled ashes from his pipe and fumbled in all his pockets for matches. Now something sporty and flashy had come over him; he carried himself a little bit like a happy boy scout, and he used exactly the language one expected of a man in his position. Had the AC exercises brain-washed him to such a degree that he had willingly accepted the recommendation by the state to all publishers that they only publish socially oriented literature? He hadn't even expressed himself in figurative terms and excused himself by hinting that the state was putting pressure on the firm because it covered the deficit. Socially oriented! He knew what the expression meant, and it was why he had entirely stopped reading the new Danish novels which all followed the same pattern. Marriage crisis in a superblock. Boredom and aggression. Economic problems. Drinking. Perhaps a would be-suicide. Then the gradual moral realization that something would have to be done about the miserable situation. The protagonist discovers that life is *the others*. What is greater than the sense of belonging? What is more beautiful than social solidarity? At their most daring, the novels usually ended with the protagonist painting his apartment in garish colors and buying her flowers, if it was a he, and making spicy dinners for him, if it was a she. The titles! *We are all together. Sunday will always come. Lose yourself, win your life.* These were the titles the libraries bought, these were the titles the booksellers exhibited in their windows; ninety per cent of Danish literature. The remaining ten per cent were made up of a couple of stubborn loners. Apart from them, there was some experimental poetry incomprehensible to anybody but the twenty students who composed it and which was kept alive because it was entirely safe and could moreover give the impression that the publishers were by no means afraid of the new, the unorthodox, the suggestive. He himself was in the middle, a loner, but not stubborn, neither socially oriented nor experimental – but with an experience out of the ordinary (one might well say): the experience of killing one's wife. But even that was not something he could write about! If he brought in a novel which began like all the others with boredom, drink and aggressions in a superblock and which did not end in joy and bubbly happiness, (but instead with everybody gouging each other's eyes out and murdering each other left, right and center), then it would be returned with the comment that his imagination probably had gone a bit overboard. They might even laugh at him, he thought and remembered the psychiatrist and his book collection. He realized that many of the novels the psychiatrist had on his shelves and which he had been particularly enthusiastic about were precisely those socially oriented novels produced in the last two, three or four years. He didn't know why he suddenly thought of that. Nor did he know why it frightened him.

'We really liked your first books, you know,' said the publisher and flexed his fingers so the knuckles cracked. 'I can even tell you that they are frequently the subject of group studies at the universities. They do give quite an accurate picture of the confusion of the late sixties and early seventies. It *was* a strange time, no doubt about it!'

'And then you didn't dictate to your writers what to write,' he said in an attempt to score points.

'Now now, none of this old-world argumentativeness,' answered the publisher. 'As though you, with your great talent for writing, should not be able to contribute greatly to socially oriented literature.'

'I suppose I'll have to go somewhere else,' he said.

'That would be a pity,' said the publisher looking happy, 'but if you change your mind, stop by.'

He didn't want to go home. On the other hand he had no idea where to go when he got back down on the street. It was late afternoon, and people were hurrying from work and towards the underground. It was raining and the sulphurous air bothered his eyes. He remembered that he still hadn't eaten, but why then wasn't he hungry? In a cafeteria he tried to force some spaghetti down his throat, but the dismal interior killed his appetite. Around him were some foreign workers, who were chased out by a guard as soon as they had eaten and had gulped down their coffee. The indefinable canned music emerging from a hidden loudspeaker increased his restlessness.

Gradually all the streets emptied. Copenhagen went to rest, put out the few remaining lights, and closed the curtains in the high-rises. The movie houses were almost empty, most restaurants had gone bankrupt years ago and only The Royal Theater still presented an occasional performance. On the boulevards various mission groups competed in their attempts to win humanity to Jesus. At one point humanity consisted of him and a drunken sailor belching in a doorway. 'May the Light of Heaven shine upon you!' a missionary shouted after him, desperately.

The Town Hall Square! Why was he walking here? Why did he walk towards the Central Station? Why did he change his mind and walk towards Tivoli? Out of habit he turned his head to read the news display on the *Politiken* building, but there was no display and no *Politiken* newspaper at all anymore. Only a huge hole in the ground and a wooden fence with a notice stating that the new social institute was being built here. Its next door neighbor, the People's Insurance Building with its twenty stories, already towered above him. A SECURE PEOPLE IS A HAPPY PEOPLE, the display on it read, making him shiver. He hurried on and finally faced the entrance to Tivoli, at the exact spot where in his dream he had been hitting Edith. He almost fainted when he thought for an instant that she was right behind him, wanting to stroke his neck. But it was an old lady out walking her decrepit poodle. She poked his shoulder and asked him for the time. Do you know who I am? he wanted to ask her, as the world kept on spinning. Do you know what I have done? Do you know that you are facing a man who killed his wife? Somebody had to listen to him, someone had to listen to his story. Perhaps the Arab on the opposite sidewalk would listen to him. Perhaps the policeman writing down the license number of a car further down the street. The world had to listen to him. The world had to understand him. 'I'm guilty!' he heard himself yell.

43

'And all I wanted to know was the time,' the little old lady said, as she disappeared across the roadway, shaking her head.

CHAPTER FOUR

'Tax withholding rate! Can't you tell that the word is much too negatively loaded?' the section chief at BLIMP asked him. And what could he answer? That he didn't think so? The word had been part of the language for decades and sounded pretty harmless! But whenever the orders came from above that a word or a phrase had to be changed, there was nothing to be done. Find an expression which makes it look as though taxes aren't something *deducted* from people's wages, but that they are part of a common *contribution* to a common fund, the section chief ended.

'Contribution rate?' he said.

'Yes, why not,' the section chief replied and clicked his ballpoint pen. Then he changed his mind suddenly: 'No, it won't work. If somebody pays eighty per cent of his earnings in taxes, that is not the same thing as saying that he is responsible for eighty per cent of the common fund. But you are usually able to crack the hard ones ... what's been wrong with you, anyway?'

'Wrong?'

'Yes, haven't you been in the hospital? That's what the Helpers at your apartment said. Nerves?'

'Yes, nerves', he said weakly and pulled some paper out of

45

his desk. When the section chief had gone he hung ten pieces of paper on the wall and began writing on them in big letters. On the first one he wrote TAX WITHHOLDING RATE. That was the minus that had to be made into a plus. On the next he wrote CONTRIBUTION RATE. Here was the right idea, but the word had the wrong meaning. SECURITY YIELD he wrote on the third piece and knew as he wrote it that it was too abstract and heavy, like flour in the mouth. Then he sat down and looked out the window. Something to do with community, with security, he thought. Security deduction? No, there it was again, the wrong idea of money being deducted. He gave up finding the right word and remained sitting where he was the rest of the morning, doing nothing. What would happen if he did nothing and got to the point where he was contributing nothing for his pay? He would be fired, but so what? He would receive social aid, he would be forced to move into a one-room apartment, but so what? Didn't he want to move anyway?

When the depression made him restless he took one of the pills the Helpers had given him when he explained that he had lost the first ones. There was an hour until the lunch meeting. Then they would all go and sit at the horseshoe-shaped vinyl table in the discussion room and criticize each other's suggestions for how negatively loaded expressions could be changed to positively loaded ones and vice versa. In the last couple of months before he went to the hospital they had all been working on changing the positively loaded expression 'home-working housewife' to a negatively loaded one: the government wanted to force all women to work in the public sector, and so it was necessary to prepare a campaign against those remaining at home. He himself had suggested calling house-wives who worked at home 'potholders', and had been praised for his idea until somebody said that the idea was too positive. It might even become attractive to be a potholder, just as it had become popular to be a 'status-woman', another expression they had debated. Finally somebody suggested the expression 'passive-woman', and it had been accepted unanimously. It was already well integrated into the language.

46

It appeared on buses, he noticed from his window ('Are *you* also tired of being a passive-woman?'). It was being used in radio and television and orders had been given that it be included in future editions of encyclopaedias and schoolbooks. In a few weeks the expressions 'home-working housewife' and 'housewife' had just about disappeared from the language. There were now only two kinds of women in Denmark, passive-women and active-women, and the aim was to make all women into active-women. This simplification of the language was the main task of BLIMP as part of the great progressive language reform (PROGLANG) which would among other things result in a new, authorized dictionary that would be distributed free to all households and in which all words would fall into two groups only: plus-words and minus-words.

'Fund share', he thought all of a sudden. He wrote the word on a piece of paper. It didn't sound bad. But even so, no. He felt his restlessless disappear, and instead he became enervated, and gave up trying to think up new ideas. On the one hand they wanted him passive and because he couldn't live with his depression he let them do it. On the other hand they demanded that he be on the ball and full of ideas. That was their problem, he decided, and vaguely heard the lunch bell ring.

He was the last to get there. Tea was being poured, beers were being opened. The three section chiefs sat on a low dais at the end of the horseshoe table and were busy presenting the monthly government reply to the institute's work. As a whole, the government was satisfied with the details of the work, but felt that a bit more speed might be desirable. Was it necessary to use weeks to find a new word or concept? Was it necessary to use eleven weeks to invent the expression 'passive-woman'? Eight weeks to change the negatively loaded expression 'old age' to the positively loaded one 'the harmonious age'? And how many weeks would it take before the bureau

47

came up with a positive expression to replace the negative one 'child certificate'?

'As far as the last item is concerned,' one of the section chiefs said, 'I think we should agree to call it a mum-and-dad-card.'

'Even though there was some opposition to the expression at our last meeting?' the other section chief said. 'Some people seemed to think it sounded too ... sentimental.'

'What difference does *that* make?' said the third section chief.

'It'll just make those who can't have the certificate even sadder,' said a girl he hadn't noticed before. She looked to be about twenty-five and was sitting by herself, drinking neither tea nor beer. Instead she was chain-smoking cigarettes and seemed clearly nervous about something or other. Perhaps it was just because she was a new arrival at the bureau, he thought.

'Those who do get it, however, will be even happier,' the first section chief said.

'That doesn't make it any better, does it?' said the girl.

She looked as though she immediately regretted saying it, and the section chiefs chose to ignore her. They quickly obtained a decision to the effect that mum-and-dad-card probably was the best expression if the idea was seriously to make the certificate popular among the population. Perhaps one might even see all those who wanted to be parents exerting themselves to such a degree that they would pass the obligatory tests without any difficulty, and then, the first section chief said to the girl, everything would be fine. All the assistants applauded the section chief, but he knew that this was an artificial enthusiasm which merely served to conceal their bad conscience. They were mostly of his own generation, old Marxists, structuralists and semiologists who had once proclaimed the revolution via 'pure' literature and had published extremely arcane periodicals; former concretists and pop artists and electronic futurists; burned-out provos and hippies and student activists and finally a few self-searching novelists like himself who had broken through in the early seventies but had stopped writing since then and were now dreaming of the comeback they knew would never happen. The Paradise Now generation. Demand-the-impossible people. Children of Mao and Marcuse. One after the other they had been forced to find work with BLIMP, but none of them dared admit they despised it – quite the contrary: they were always jolly and bright and pretended that the task of rationalizing the language was creative as well as progressive.

The only one who seemed different was the girl who had dared to object. What was her problem? Had the Helpers just taken her child certificate? Or did she want children but didn't feel she would pass the obligatory tests? And why was she looking at him all the time? Did he seem just as odd in her eyes as she did in his? Was it possible to tell that he was on drugs? Her nervousness alerted him and he tried to move so that he would not always be caught by her glance. Instead a former concretist looked at him. He knew him from the time they had a debate in the papers concerning 'The expulsion of Man from art'. At the time they could not meet without throwing concepts and theories at one another, and after one discussion they had even come to blows. Later they were reconciled and now they only spoke in artificially confidential tones about nothing at all when they met. About the difficulty of not drinking and of keeping the payment orders at bay. About the boredom of existence and new spicy herbs for one's window box.

'You look tired, Torben.'

'Tired?' he asked dully.

'Yes, you've got black circles under your eyes!'

'I don't think so,' he said.

'Yes, you have, Torben.'

'Circles under my eyes?'

'Yes. Look, is something wrong?'

'No, what would be wrong!?' he answered angrily and got up.

He had to go to the men's room to put cold water on his face. He hurried out of the discussion room, and even though he knew that he was only allowed one a day he had already taken out the bottle of pills from his pocket.

He gradually worked his way up to five or six pills a day. Time no longer existed for him; he was usually one or two hours late for work and he often fell asleep in his office during the afternoon. On one occasion he even went to sleep on the floor and only woke up the next morning when a charwoman pushed him with her mop. He forgot to wash and shave and his clothes got dirty. People didn't matter to him anymore; he didn't answer when spoken to and ran into them in the corridors when they wouldn't step aside. The bureau, the underground, the streets of Copenhagen – he was unable to tell where he was at any given time. If he was on the underground he sometimes thought he was in the discussion room at the bureau, so that he stayed on the train way past the station he was supposed to get out at and did not come to until a trainman at the end of the line rapped on the window to get him out. If he was at the office, he thought that he was in the superblock and that he only needed to press the button in the hallway to make the Helpers bring more pills, and only when he got up to open the door and saw one of the employees of the bureau, did he realize where he was. Then he became frightened because he could make such a mistake and he would pretend to be working by pinning more pieces of paper on the wall and writing TAX WITHHOLDING RATE on all of them. It was at just such a time, when he was relatively clear-headed, that the section chief knocked on the door and shortly after entered.

'I'm sorry,' was the first thing he said.

'Sorry about what?' he asked, not caring.

The section chief looked wonderingly from one piece of paper to the other and scratched the tip of his nose:

'It wasn't my decision,' he said, 'I always valued you highly.'

'But?'

'To put it bluntly: you aren't considered to be quite the sort of person ... the bureau needs. Recently you haven't been approachable at all, and you don't seem ...'

The section chief straddled the chair and looked straight at him:

'Tell me, what *is* the matter with you?'

He could no longer quell a sudden rage that overwhelmed him. Everybody asked him what was the matter. Now they had been asking for days, for weeks, for months, and they would go on asking him, year in, year out. What is wrong with you, Torben. You don't look well, Torben. You have dark circles under your eyes, Torben. And every time he would have to sit there and look at the floor and fumble with a pen or a matchbox and answer that nothing was wrong with him, he was absolutely fine, and it couldn't be right that he had dark circles under his eyes. No more of that! From now on he would grab all of those who asked him in the same way that he now seized the section chief:

'I feel great!' he shouted and shook the section chief. 'I've never felt better!'

Then they both fell to the floor and he was just about to take the section chief's head and bang it against the floor. He kept hearing himself shout that he was fine, that he was absolutely all right, that he had never felt better. Then his rage gradually disappeared and instead he felt sick. He let go of the section chief, ran into the corridor and took the elevator to the fourth floor. He didn't know why he did it. He had nothing to do on the fourth floor.

Then he pressed another button, and shortly afterwards the elevator stopped at the second floor. He hurried out in order not to keep on going down, and then he came to the canteen. He got hold of a pot of strong tea, but when he had sat down and put sugar and milk in it he didn't feel like drinking it. He just wanted to sleep. For ten, twenty, forty hours at a stretch. Then somebody sat down next to him. It was the girl who had objected to calling the child certificate a mum-and-dad-card. She still looked sad and chain-smoked cigarettes.

'Why aren't you drinking your tea?' she asked.

For once there was somebody who wasn't asking him what was wrong with him. He looked at the girl in amazement.

'I just want to sleep,' he said and wondered why she wasn't surprised that he was answering her like that. She rather looked as though that was just the answer she was expecting. She put one hand on his shoulder:

'You can sleep at my place.'

He awoke to an aroma of coffee and fresh rolls. The sun was shining in through a window and promising spring at long last. He didn't know how long he had slept, he didn't know where he was, and suddenly he started up and threw aside the eiderdown so that it overturned a bedside table tray with breakfast of coffee and rolls. The coffee ran over the floor and one of the rolls rolled under a closet. He was in a light and friendly room with posters from Sicily and Corsica on the walls, lots of flowers in the windowsills and a bookshelf with some novels he guessed were probably of the socially trendy sort. He remained sitting for a while and looking around. Then something slowly became clear to him. The section chief had come into his office with the news that he was fired. The elevator had taken him up and down. The canteen, where he had the strong tea he couldn't drink and the girl who had sat down next to him. He remembered everything suddenly in great detail and therefore he wasn't surprised when the girl came in a moment later and asked him if he had slept well.

'I feel rested as never before,' he said and apologized because he had overturned the tray.

'Never mind,' she said and picked up the rolls. 'That can happen to anybody.'

'What time is it?' he asked.

'Way after noon,' she said. 'You've slept for two days!'

'Where are we?'

'In Dragør,' she said.

He looked out the window and all he could see was an

endless superblock. The sun went behind some clouds.

'Are the trees dying out here as well?' he asked.

'Don't ask me that,' she said, 'I'd rather not think about it.'

Shortly after that he was sitting on the edge of the bed. She gave him his clothes. They were clean and had been ironed. Even his shoes had been polished.

'That's too much!' he said.

'Nonsense,' she answered.

'Why are you doing this for me?'

'Because I like you,' she answered. 'I liked you from the first day I saw you.'

'But I'm a murderer!' he was just about to exclaim. I've killed my wife. And it wasn't an accident. I did it on purpose. I hit her in the face, in the stomach, in her kidneys, on her flanks. And later I took her head and hammered it against the wall and the floor. I didn't even stop when the blood began running from her mouth. He wanted to frighten her by telling her in the smallest detail what had happened, but when it came to the point he couldn't really open his mouth. The words got stuck in his throat, his neck hurt and he felt most of all like taking a pill but decided that he would try to do without them for a few days. He broke open a roll and put butter on it, and when the girl went into the kitchen and came back shortly after with fresh coffee he only wanted to talk normally with her – about why she had been so gloomy the times he had seen her at the bureau, whether she lived by herself, was divorced or merely single, whether she had any children or wanted any. Who was she?

'I don't even know your name,' he said.

'Bridgit,' she answered.

'Do you live alone?'

'Doesn't it look that way?' she replied quietly.

He didn't have time to ask any more questions. The girl said she had to go visit her mother and would be gone most of the afternoon but would be back by six so they could have dinner together. She spoke to him as though they had known each other for years and it was the most natural thing in the world

53

that he should be lying in her bed and she should serve him coffee. She told him to make himself at home. There were lots of books and magazines for him to read. There was a tv and a record-player. And there was even some nature left in the Kongelunden park if he wanted to go for a walk – he could borrow her bicycle if he wanted to go there, it was in the basement, unlocked, she ended and picked up the last roll, put the coffee cup and the pot on the tray and carried it out. In the doorway she turned around to face him and smiled distantly.

Who was she? He kept asking himself that most of the afternoon. She evidently devoured socially oriented novels and *Home and Person* and all the other weeklies and monthlies with their thousand and one pieces of advice on how to find happiness, but did that tell him anything at all about her, really? She raised flowers and herbs in all her window-boxes, but did that really reveal anything other than that she also sought a more beautiful world than the one around them? Perhaps she had been married, but nothing indicated that she had had children. The apartment was painfully neat and gave no impression of having had many male visitors. He couldn't find a single bottle of wine or liquor. What had she done before she was hired by the bureau? Was she from the provinces or from Copenhagen? The only characteristic thing about her was her enormous consumption of cigarettes – she bought them by the carton and piled them up everywhere so she could reach them quickly. She must smoke at least three packs a day, he calculated by counting the stubs in a ceramic ashtray which oddly enough, she had forgotten to empty.

By the time he had just about decided to go for a walk in the remains of the park she suddenly returned. She had had a fight with her mother, she explained evasively and immediately went to the kitchen and began preparing food.

'Are we eating already?' he asked in surprise.

'No, not until six or seven o'clock,' she replied, 'but I love to make good food, and it always takes time.'

He didn't understand why she kept on behaving as though she had nobody but him to think about. While she stayed in the kitchen he threw himself on a couch in the living-room and looked at some of the issues of *Home and Person*. When he reached the one Edith had been reading the night he killed her everything returned to him. He threw the magazine across the room and got up, walking restlessly about until he almost decided to give up and take a pill, when the girl came to him with a bottle of vermouth and two glasses (he still couldn't think of her as Bridgit).

'Come, let's sit down,' she said and pointed to two safari chairs on either side of a marble chessboard. 'Would you like to hear some music?'

'I'm not in the mood for music.'

'Why not?' she asked, sitting down.

That was the first time she had pressed him at all. In a moment she would probably ask what was the matter with him. But instead of frightening her by seizing her the way he had attacked the section chief he felt a need to confide in her. Here was a person, at last, who would listen to him and understand him. She would not be able to forgive, but she would listen, and that would be enough. Perhaps she would even listen to his story again and again until one day he got back the strength to live with his guilt. But she didn't ask him anything else. After she had been sitting for a while twirling the stem of her glass between her fingers she suddenly began crying:

'I can't have children,' she said.

She lit a cigarette with another:

'They say I'm not suited to be a mother ... but I still want to have a child secretly ... many of my friends do too ...'

He put down his glass and quite forgot that he had wanted to confide in her. He tried to seem calm. Now he had to listen.

'And then I thought ... because I like you ... that maybe you'd want to be the father ...'

He started.

'I mean without any commitments,' she said. 'I won't tell

anyone that it's you.'

'Why can't you get the certificate?' he asked.

'Because they say that I'm unreliable and don't do my work well. And it's true! I'm not good enough to get a mum-and-dad-card! But I want a child anyway!'

He was angry that she accepted her own worthlessness without question and that she already referred to the child certificate as the mum-and-dad-card. She obviously didn't have the spirit of protest he had thought at first.

'Of course you're good enough!' he said sternly. 'Nothing's wrong with *you*!'

She brightened:

'So you'll be the father then. Now I'll go and fix dinner.'

She jumped up from her chair and happily poured him another vermouth and smoothed down her dress. He kept on looking at her.

'I'm a murderer.'

She didn't look surprised at all. It was as though he could have said that he was a baker, or a housepainter. Nevertheless he told her everything, to the last detail, the blood running from Edith's mouth. He stopped and drank. Then he emphasized – feeling unsure about himself and the girl and the whole situation – :

'I'm guilty of a *murder*.'

Now she looked at him angrily.

'Why do you say such nonsense?'

'It's true nevertheless.'

'There's no such thing as guilt anymore, you know that ...'

Something censorious, pedantic, tight-lipped (almost like an old-fashioned piano teacher) had come over her:

'It's always the circumstances that dictate our actions.'

Those were the very words he feared. He heard a thousand psychologists and social workers speaking through her mouth, and he realized with utter clarity that she really was convinced that she was living in the best of all worlds. Perhaps she felt depressed momentarily that the child certificate was now being called a mum-and-dad-card, but she quickly accepted it and did not doubt for a second that she did not deserve it. If she wanted to be a mother, it was in the same way as a child who wants some forbidden toy. Only her unlimited naiveté kept her from realizing that the child would be forcibly aborted if the Helpers discovered that she was pregnant within the first three months. It would be put up for adoption even if she was allowed to complete the pregnancy. Her excessive use of cigarettes showed that she probably did not always think that everything was as it should be, but then she had her socially oriented novels to tell her what was what. And so would her innumerable issues of *Home and Person*, her group dynamics, her AC exercises and – who knows – perhaps a coming course in how to raise bonsai trees. For a moment he felt as though he were in the same room with Edith, the Edith who really couldn't see anything wrong in the fact that it now was Hans Christian Andersen's turn to be demythologized. A panic gripped him; the fear that everything would be repeated but in a slightly different and more devilish way: he already heard himself yelling at the girl, while he beat her: 'Take it easy! I'm not killing you! It's just the *cir—cum—stances*!'

He put down his glass and got up. His stomach heaved and he felt the veins in his throat expanding.

'Are you going?' she asked, afraid.

'How could you think anything else?' he replied and went towards the door.

She ran after him. She started to weep again:

'But I like you a lot!' she cried after him as he ran down the stairs.

Dragør. Or what was once the charming village of Dragør, he thought as he passed between rows of blocks to find the sea which he heard somewhere in the distance. It was getting dark, and it must be Sunday since nobody seemed to be on their way home from work. At the same time a wind began blowing, and an all-pervading stench of sulphur and chemicals was carried in over land. When he reached the end of the rows of houses he saw the sea on both sides, apparently no different from how it had looked during all the millennia it yielded food for humanity. He reached the waterfront and sat down on a rock, trying to endure the stench and the knowledge that only a few strange worm-like, maggot-white creatures had survived deep down under the waves.

CHAPTER FIVE

He knew that it would be pointless, but nevertheless he went to the bureau that issued and recalled mum-and-dad-cards to find out whether he had a chance of ever getting Jasper back. He got the reply that no action could be taken in the matter before he returned his mum-and-dad-card. 'But what if I don't send it back?' he asked. 'That will be the worse for you,' was the reply, 'because then you'll have to pay ever higher fines until you do.' – 'But suppose I've lost it?' he asked further. 'Well, then you can certainly never have it back; isn't that obvious?' was the reply.

He became stubborn:

'What about those people who lose their cards even though they have a right to them?'

'Are you going to continue?' the lady behind the desk asked. She was around sixty and looked like the type one would find in any office; an obedient, powdered, bejewelled servant of authority who would dispassionately handle all cases which came to her, whether they concerned patents for developing solar energy or imprisoning minorities in concentration camps. Now it happened to be children. Some people were allowed to have them, and some people weren't, that was how simple it was, and she would see to it that no human feelings disturbed the order which reigned in her accounts.

'Do you have children of your own?' he asked her.

'I can't see that it has anything to do with your case,' she replied, totally unperturbed.

'Can I put a final question?'

'A *final* question, yes.'

'What reason is given for my son's being kept from me?'

'That you are unbalanced. That's what it says: unbalanced . . .'

She closed the file on his case, tired of talking with him. He remained standing for some time in front of the desk until he was told to leave the room as there were several people outside waiting their turn. She had already used up too much time on him. An elderly, friendly-looking man had entered the room. The atmosphere suddenly changed. He guessed that the elderly man was probably in charge of the department or something, and before he had really thought about it he was addressing him with a complaint about the treatment he had been given. As the older man listened to him sympathetically, the lady behind the desk became frightened and apologized that she had been so impatient. But there were so many people who came in to complain.

'Aren't you the person who wrote . . .'

'Yes, I am,' he replied before the older man had the chance to mention the titles of the books.

'What a pleasure to meet you! Do you want to step into my office for a moment?'

It turned out that the older man was in charge of the department. He was a civil servant and a lover of literature. Probably the last survivor of the old school, member of the Resistance during the German Occupation and product of a childhood in bourgeois Østerbro in the thirties. If he still voted at elections he would probably vote for the Old Liberals or the Center Party, but it was likely enough that he had decided, as had most everybody else, that putting marks on a ballot every four years had very little significance, if any. Just as he had given up reading recent novels.

'I do prefer the kind of literature which sows doubt in your mind,' he said and looked at him amiably. 'The kind of books you wrote. How sad that you stopped. But tell me, what is your business here?'

'Well, that reads like an old kind of novel,' he said, 'The Big Brother kind of science fiction.'

'In other words: your mum-and-dad-card?'

'Yes. I want to know what the reason is that it has been taken from me ... or rather: that my son has been taken from me.'

The director of the office sat down behind his old-fashioned desk and called outside for the file on his case. Almost immediately the old lady came in with it and almost curtsied as she handed it over.

'Yes, well, it says here that you are considered to be ... unbalanced,' the director said after he had looked at the papers.

'It must say more,' he said.

The director shook his head gently and offered him a cigarette.

'But I committed a murder! It must say that I am guilty of my wife's death.'

'Aren't you exaggerating a little?' the director asked. But he didn't really seem to believe his own words. His glance wavered, and after a bit he suddenly spoke.

'All right, since it's you. Strictly in confidence, it does say that you caused the decease of your wife ...'

'In other words: I'm guilty of murder.'

'It doesn't say that ...'

'My boy has been taken from me! Right? That has to be a kind of punishment. Right? Punishment you get if you're guilty. Right?'

'That certainly is one way of looking at it,' the director said, 'but ...'

'But?'

'Punishment and guilt are not concepts we use any more.'

'I've heard that a hundred times,' he said, 'but what do you call it when my son has been taken from me?'

'Precautions.'

'*You* don't believe that one, do you?'

'What do you want me to do?' the director asked, sadly. 'I agree with you more than you think. But that's the way things are. I see here that you have worked in the Bureau of Language Improvement, so that you should know better than I how words and concepts can change their meaning from one day to the next and even disappear altogether in favor of new ones, which express the same thing of course, only in a more flexible manner ...'

'Flexible?' he snarled. 'In the old days, when you were punished, you knew that it would last for a certain length of time. If you were put in jail for four years, you went for four years; maybe you were even paroled after two or three years. Now I'm punished by having my son taken away, but I have no idea if I'll ever get him back. Because this isn't punishment. Because I'm not guilty. I'm just unbalanced. Is that what you call flexible?'

'As I said to you before: I understand you. I agree with you. Don't blame me.'

'Why did you take this job if you can't be criticized?'

The director got up and began walking up and down the room. Something uncertain, inhibiting, had come over him, and it was as though he felt there were strangers in the room who could listen to their conversation. He wanted to say something, but didn't feel he dared. That was how it seemed. Then he went to the window and looked out over a grey and dusty city which was still waiting for spring. He pulled his coat tighter as though he were freezing:

'How can I reply except by repeating the usual chant: if-I-didn't-have-this-job-someone-else-would-have-it. I have a certain standard of living, I have children in higher education, and I'm not fit at all for anything except civil service. I'd like nothing better than to be in control of ...'

'Circumstances,' he interrupted.

'Yes, circumstances ...'

The director became more and more unhappy and seemed

on the point of breaking down at any moment. Nervously and with much stuttering he said that the only thing that meant anything to him was to be able to read his books. He had a collection of over four thousand volumes, mostly Russian literature, some English essays, a complete set of the works of Molière, and then, of course, all the important Danish fiction from the middle of last century until ... 'yes, until your work,' he added, as though it were a soothing balm for his wound to emphasize once again that he had read him.

The director paused briefly and looked at him very apologetically.

'Don't ask me any more,' he added. 'We're in the same boat.'

'All I want is to know that I'm guilty,' he said.

'I'll help you as far as I can,' the director said and became the competent bureaucrat again. He sat down behind his desk, authoritative and secure:

'If you write a letter to the department here explaining your case, I'll do what I can to see to it that your papers state that you are guilty of the murder of your wife. But I cannot promise anything, and I certainly cannot guarantee that it will be admitted that it is a punishment that your son has been taken away ... in the sense that this punishment will expire at some point and you will get him back. It will be a major matter, and I shall first have to talk to the Helpers where you live and the psychiatrists at the hospital, where, according to these papers, you were kept after your ... deed. – But, as I said, I'll do what I can.'

The director saw him to the door. As he was walking down a long corridor he was suddenly overcome by exhaustion. He could not understand where he had got the energy to go to the directorate and to be so tough with the director. It had to be part of the rage he had felt for some days after he had let himself be led home by the girl from Dragør, a rage which was due to the ease with which everybody surrendered to the system. He would never be like that girl, he had vowed, but now he felt the last drops of protest seeping from him as from a punctured balloon, and when the elevator didn't come for a

63

long time he thought of just sitting down on the floor and staring straight ahead. Then a woman came up to him. Her face was haggard and tears were streaming down her cheeks:

'I want my children back!' she shouted in his face.

'You're mistaken,' he said, 'I don't even work here.'

'You just don't want to admit it,' she answered and spat in his face.

Instead of feeling angry he felt sympathy for the woman, but as she continued to berate him and started to hit him he hurried into the elevator when it finally arrived. He wiped the spit from his face, rode down and went out into the street without knowing where to go.

He had been moved into a one-room apartment in the super-block. As he had continued to avoid going to the post office with the payment orders for rent, extra taxes and the innumerable insurance forms, kept on throwing the notices into the garbage chute, and failed to be home at the times the Helpers said they would come to talk to him about economy and management, they had lost patience with him. One morning the Helpers let themselves into the apartment and began to remove all the furniture while he slowly came to. He put on a bathrobe and protested their procedure in vain. He tried to stop the Helpers from carrying out the furniture, but then they told him that they would call the police if he did not restrain himself and that in any case he shouldn't get angry with them, as they were simply following orders. By that afternoon he was installing himself in the new apartment which was not much more than twelve by eighteen feet plus a toilet and a small kitchenette. The furniture for which there was no longer any room had been driven away to storage somewhere; he didn't know where, they just gave him a phone number to call. In the evening he already felt as though he had lived there for a long time. Most of the furniture which he had kept was his own from before he met Edith. The rug was from his early school days, his desk with its scores of cup marks, pen drawings, scribbled phone numbers and marks from the typewriter, was almost as old. There were also his textbooks from the university, some files and the easy chair which had been re-upholstered at least five times, (every time Edith had seen a new pattern in *Home and Person*) but which he had had since the mid-sixties when he inherited it from his grandmother. Only the bed, some kitchenware and a couple of flower-pots dated from the marriage. When he had hung curtains and sheets over the windows to be free of the sight of concrete, he might for a moment think that time had stood still for the last twenty or twenty-five years and he was still in the room he had had in his parents' house in the sixties. From now on he would even be taken care of to the extent that he had been before he left home. Once a week he was to go to the Helpers to receive a small portion of his social aid as pocket money, while they kept the rest so they could pay his running expenses. He received a permanent card for the nearest canteen. Once a month he would be given two hundred crowns for laundry and new clothes, and every six months he would get five hundred crowns for furniture and any other necessities. He was free to arrange his time as he wished, apart from two weekly visits to a psychiatrist in the superblock and compulsory attendance at group dynamics sessions and AC exercises. However, he had to call the Helpers if he left his apartment for more than two days. And if he suddenly began making money at odd jobs here and there he was to report it at once.

He tried to see the best in the situation. He would never again have a bad conscience because of his demoralizing work at BLIMP. He would never again have to run to the post office at the last minute with piles of payment orders; he could sleep when he pleased and do what he pleased when he wasn't sleeping; he could play solitaire, do jigsaw puzzles, play darts, collect stamps, take bicycle rides to the last nature spots, find new friends, maybe even a new girl. He only had himself to worry about, and some time or other he might even start the novels he had been planning in the hospital – if nobody would publish them he could at least write them for his own gratification and hope that one day, if society changed in some way, they would be pulled out of anonymity and be proof that the creative imagination could survive decades of conformism. But he couldn't keep his optimism for more than a few minutes at a time, and after the first night in the new apartment, when he awoke half a dozen times from variations on the same nightmares – Edith pleading with him to stop beating her to death and Jasper begging for him to come and get him away from wherever he was – he fought an almost impossible battle to keep off the pills. Gradually he became obsessed with the idea that he had to find the cemetery where Edith was buried and the place where Jasper was, whether he was in a state school or with private people. His in-laws would know, of course, where Edith was buried, but dare he call them? Dare he hear his mother-in-law's voice? Not to mention his father-in-law's. No, it would be best if he called one cemetery office after another and pretended to be one of Edith's childhood friends who had returned from Japan and now wanted to put a flower on her grave. Or maybe he could kill two birds with one stone: Jasper *had* to know where she was buried; he had probably been at the funeral. Or had they told him that she wasn't dead at all? That she had gone abroad and that his dad had gone after her? Was that what they would tell a child? Or would they just say that she had fallen ill? And he? What about him? That he had fallen ill too? He suddenly began wondering if Jasper might have been a witness to the murder. Could he possibly, through the fog of alcohol and blood, have got a glimpse of Jasper in the living-room, weeping and holding his hands over his face? Had Jasper perhaps even tried to protect his mother, and had he brutally pushed him aside so that he only dared throw himself across his mother's lifeless body when the Helpers broke into the apartment to stop the insanity? If it were true that Jasper had witnessed the murder he would probably never speak with him again even if he found him! But why should it be true? Why did this picture of Jasper in his pyjamas covering his face with his hands suddenly appear in his mind? Delusions? Exhaustion? Fear?

Questions continued to bother him, and he began wandering aimlessly around between the concrete buildings. He ran up and down as though physical exertion would help, but even if he ran so far that the sulphurous air tore his lungs and his heart burst into his throat he could not drive the image of Jasper in his night-clothes weeping from his mind. And one day after a run he looked in the phone book and wrote down the numbers of all the schools in Copenhagen on a piece of paper next to the numbers of the cemetery offices he already had noted down in a neat column. This time he would pretend that he was an uncle or something, and if it turned out that Jasper was attending one of the schools and hadn't been sent to a boarding school in Jutland he would stand outside the gate and wait for school to be over, and if Jasper then came to meet him, but turned away as soon as he saw who he was and ran across the road to the opposite sidewalk he would know that Jasper knew. On the one hand he hoped that Jasper knew nothing, he really hoped that he hadn't seen anything. On the other hand he would be the only witness that he was guilty of Edith's death and did not simply 'cause her decease' (an invention of the Helpers?). He felt his mind spinning: Jasper was to give evidence that he was guilty so he could be told that it was a punishment that he had been taken from him and expect to have him back after the punishment expired, except Jasper wouldn't want to come back because he would be terrified for life by what he had seen.

No, Jasper probably knew nothing. If he wanted to make sure that he would be declared guilty he would have to write that letter to the director. Things had to be done in the right sequence. First the letter to the director. Then the calls to the cemetery office. And finally the systematic attempt to find Jasper.

He sat down at his desk, put a pile of paper at his left hand, pens and pencil at his right and the typewriter in the middle, which he dusted off before using – his classical ritual whenever he was going to write. It took him some time to find the right introduction to the letter. He tried various polite phrases until he finally rejected all drafts and went right to the heart of the matter. *I am guilty of murder* he began, and then he described the night it happened, how Edith and he had attended the AC exercises, how they had come home tired, how they had begun getting on one another's nerves, how they had started fighting. He avoided describing the reason for their fight (his suspicion that she had begun believing that the pedagogical measures were somehow good and useful, a suspicion which was confirmed by her reaction to the tv program about Hans Christian Andersen): there was no reason to antagonize the educational authorities who would inevitably become involved in his case. He strongly emphasized, however, what a bad husband he had been for many years, that he had refused any housework, that he had gone out on the town on many occasions and that he had seventeen different mistresses here and there. It had been his purpose to get a divorce, but when Edith resisted and – when he insisted – threatened to reveal certain unpleasant truths about him (which ones? he would have to invent some for the purposes of replying to interrogations at the directorate) he saw no way out except killing her in the hope that it would look like an accident. Now the time had come for him to tell the truth. And if he were not believed and declared guilty he would have to write a book giving all the details, a book which would inevitably cause a great deal of attention. In the directorate they would not know about his problems in getting accepted as a writer again, but the mere thought of a book criticizing the system would be enough to frighten them, he thought.

He smiled when he had finished the letter and hurried down to the nearest mailbox to send it off before he began having second thoughts and correcting it endlessly. After a quick meal in the new canteen – which was arranged exactly like the one he had used before, with neon lighting, unpainted concrete walls, vinyl tables and the usual indeterminate canned music from hidden loudspeakers – he went for a long walk. For the first time in many months he felt in balance, as though he had finally caught on to a solid thread. Perhaps they would say that the explanation in his letter did not coincide with the explanation he had given at the state hospital, but he shouldn't have any trouble convincing them that only now did he dare admit how premeditated and brutal his action had been. His case would quickly become a case of principle, and he would become proof that it was possible for the individual to fight the system. Perhaps months would pass before they declared him guilty. And certainly more months would pass before they dared admit that it was a punishment that Jasper had been taken from him. And only in four or five years could he hope to get Jasper back, when they decided that he had been punished enough. But time wasn't important. He had nothing but time, and when he had found Jasper he would use it to be with him secretly as much as possible and tell him that he needn't feel bad about it. He would take him to the zoo or take him for a drive across the Big Belt Bridge and take him out to a cake-shop in Malmø and gradually initiate him into the world which would await him when he grew up. He would tell him how he would be among the first who would go exploring in space and settle new worlds and create new, free societies close to nature, where there were plenty of fish and forests with lots of animals and under a sky which did not consist of dust and sulphur and ammonia fumes.

Suddenly he realized that he was standing outside the windows of his old apartment. Light shone from them all. What sort of people had moved in? Probably a young couple without knowledge of what had happened in the apartment some months before. He thought of the tree with its branches just outside the living-room window, and he couldn't stop himself from going over to it to see whether it had really died or not. He reached up to touch one of the lower twigs, but couldn't reach it. Then he found a piece of wood which he threw up among the branches until a twig fell at his feet. It bore a bud – a single bud. It really was as though everything had got a new meaning this evening.

*   *   *

A few days later a letter arrived from the director saying that they wanted to see him. He shaved carefully, found some nice clothes and took the underground to the center of the city. From the station he took a taxi to the directorate, and was ushered in at once.

'Your letter has been read,' the director said and asked him to sit down. The director paused and looked for his file in a pile of papers on his desk. He seemed more curt than the last time, but not decidedly unfriendly.

'The view that you caused the death of your wife has been abandoned,' the director finally said when he had found the file. 'It is believed ...'

The director put on his glasses and examined the file. Then he took off his glasses and looked directly at him:

'... that an accident occurred.'

'An accident?'

His mouth went dry.

'It is supposed that your wife simply fell down in the hall-way and that she struck the back of her head in such a way that ...'

He felt like getting up, reaching across the desk, tearing the file from the director's hands telling him that this was surely the most fantastic nonsense he'd ever heard.

'Does this mean I get my son back then?' he asked.

'I'm afraid not,' the director replied.

'But ... if an accident occurred, if my wife fell and struck her head in such a way that ...'

'As I said last time: please do not blame me,' the director said.

He began shaking all over as the director continued to regard him apologetically.

'What reason is given for keeping my son from me now?'

'You are regarded as being unbalanced,' the director said, looking away.

CHAPTER SIX

For over a week the psychiatrist who had taken care of him refused to talk to him. He had called the hospital a number of times, but each time he was told that the doctor was not to be reached, whether he called in the morning or in the afternoon. Even in the evening, using the psychiatrist's home number: either a maid or his wife took the phone and as soon as they heard his name, he could detect whispering in the background and then the reply that the doctor was busy and could he please call during the regular hours of consultation. He considered using a false name, but his fear that the psychiatrist would merely use this as an excuse to break off every connection with him was too deep; so he finally decided to go see him in person.

Three times he took the underground to the hospital, walked through the park and greeted the patients, some of whom recognized him while others still walked around with their eyes to the ground. He enjoyed seeing the lawns again, the pavilions, the small lakes with birds and the trees which were some of the last trees in Copenhagen and its environs not to have suffered from root poisoning and which were all budding. He looked towards Happiness Park a few times and envied the deeply insane who could live there exactly as they wished, write books and have them published, make speeches, pass new laws in parliament, perform plays and put up easels under the trees. Then he reached the waiting room and began looking through the various colored weeklies, but when the secretary had taken his name the first two times exactly the same thing happened: she disappeared and returned shortly after with the information that the doctor could only see patients with an appointment. Could he have an appointment then? No, he could not, the doctor's calendar was filled for a year at least. The third time he sat in the waiting room the secretary simply refused to talk to him. And then he decided that he would shadow the psychiatrist on a day he was visiting the city and then contact him somewhere where he would not slip away. He found difficulty in dispelling the notion that the psychiatrist (or doctor or whatever his title was) was part of a conspiracy to drive him mad. But he refused to believe it and tried to convince himself that the psychiatrist simply had other things than him to think about and that only a series of accidents had prevented him from being able to see him. When he followed him and caught up with him at a cafeteria or on a street-corner everything would be cleared up, and the psychiatrist would happily recall their long conversations about philosophy and ethics and would naturally agree that Edith had not died as the result of an accident at all. They wouldn't even have to discuss the question of guilt; he would not upset the psychiatrist by mentioning it so that he would not start talking about an eye for an eye. The psychiatrist just had to tell him this one thing: It is true that you killed your wife.

He waited a few days by the main entrance to the hospital from early morning to late evening, and hoped desperately that the psychiatrist did not drive to and from the area. Now and then he would go to a hot dog stand or buy some biscuits and chocolate at the nearest market, but only to hurry back to the group of trees he had chosen as his vantage point. But the psychiatrist still did not appear, so he changed tactics and took up a position behind a tree near his house. He often saw him leaving the house, walking down the marble stairs and across the lawn, and he thought that nothing would be easier than to catch up with him before he disappeared into one of the hospital buildings; but on the other hand the psychiatrist might then turn him away by saying that he was much too busy to concern himself with his case. It would be best if he contacted him away from the hospital grounds. One evening what he had waited for finally happened: the psychiatrist came down the marble stairs, not wearing his usual lab coat, but a raincoat; he crossed the lawn and disappeared in the direction of the exit. He hurried after him but made sure to keep his distance. Everything went as though it were planned: the psychiatrist passed the parking area outside the hospital grounds, chose the road leading towards the underground, disappeared down the stairs to the platform and got into a train going to the center of the city. As he did not want him to know that he had shadowed him, he got into another car and waited until the next time the train stopped. Then he got out, walked distractedly past the window where the psychiatrist was sitting, pretended that he couldn't decide whether to go into the smokers' or the non-smokers' compartment, and finally chose the smokers' where the psychiatrist occupied the hindmost seat facing the sliding door. Did he try to make himself invisible? Was he trying to change places so as to be facing away from him? Was he surreptitiously trying to pull his cap down over his eyes and hide his face behind his hand? Fortunately there were only a few people in the compartment, should any trouble occur. But why should it? Why this fear that the psychiatrist was part of a conspiracy or something? Finally he took courage and went into the compartment and sat down right across from him:

'I've been trying to get hold of you for the past two weeks,' was the first (and most stupid?) thing he could think of saying.

'Yes, I hear you've been calling a number of times,' the psychiatrist answered drily. 'But you must understand that I'm very busy.'

'It's not a very big problem,' he said, 'it's about ...'

He stopped, became nervous, felt that he was getting involved in something he couldn't really get himself out of. And it was all so simple! But the psychiatrist was clearly doing whatever he could to keep his distance and looked around the compartment distractedly, as though he were simply an interfering fellow-traveller.

'It concerns my wife's death,' he said, finally holding the psychiatrist's attention.

'I see.'

'They tell me it was an accident; they tell me that I didn't kill her, that she simply fell over in the hallway and struck the back of her head ...'

'But then what's the problem?' the psychiatrist said, pulling his cap further down over his eyes and getting ready to leave the compartment as soon as the train reached another station.

'*That's* the problem', he said quietly.

'I don't understand ...'

'You know that it's not true that my wife fell over in the hallway! You know that I killed her!'

'Back to that again!' the psychiatrist said in a hard voice.

'What do you mean?'

'I thought we discussed that question the last time – when you refused to understand that you were free to return to society.'

'I no longer want to know that I'm guilty,' he said, 'I just want you to witness that I *did* it!'

'You really can't ask me to testify to something I didn't see. Excuse me.'

The psychiatrist got up and rushed out as soon as the train stopped. He had the feeling that the psychiatrist got into another car, and three stations later he saw him, sure enough, passing by on the platform. Their eyes met for a moment, and it was as though the psychiatrist was regarding him in an entirely new way, curiously, in an interested way but without sympathy. It was as though he were an experimental animal in a glass cage; one of the mice that the psychiatrist had been talking about which couldn't escape and wound up biting

74

itself, losing its fur, dying. He jumped up, and suddenly it was all clear to him; the curious, coldly examining glance of the psychiatrist had revealed everything to him. But when he got out on the platform the psychiatrist had already disappeared. He wasn't on his way up the stairs. He wasn't visible anywhere outside the station. He jumped back down the stairs and ran back as fast as he could and reached the platform just as the train started moving. He looked in all the windows and thought that he definitely saw the psychiatrist in one of them, but then it seemed that he was also sitting in another compartment, and yet another, and when the train had disappeared into the tunnel he had to sit down on a bench to clear his head. Somewhere a rat darted across the tracks. On the platform opposite some leather-jacketed thugs were threatening some foreign workers. The hands on all the clocks jumped ahead one minute so the time was exactly eleven.

After he had looked at the rat trying to hide itself under some rocks for a while, and knowing that he was too cowardly to do anything about the thugs who were now forcing the foreign workers out on to the very end of the platform, he got up and slowly walked up the stairs. It was dark when he emerged. Around him he saw dozens of superblocks and after he had been walking for some time up and down streets below identical sets of neon lights and seeing hundreds of parked cars and thousands of tv-reflecting windows, he realized that he hadn't the least idea where he was. He hadn't even looked at the name of the station where he had got out. He knew that he still must be northeast of the city center, but none of the new street-names meant anything at all to him. Not even the cemetery which suddenly appeared, in the darkness between the superblocks, resembling a bombed-out area, was familiar.

At first he didn't feel like visiting it. But after circling around it for an hour or so he felt drawn by it to such an extent that he found himself climbing the fence after having examined all the gates and doors and finding them locked. And he immediately went through the lanes looking for new graves. He found ten, but why would she be here? She might be buried anywhere in

Copenhagen or even in the provinces. The best way of finding her grave would still be to call the cemetery offices. Nevertheless he remained in the cemetery listening to the wind sighing through the tattered bushes and whirling faded flowers, twigs and a few old newspapers into the air. Here was something resembling peace. Here he could imagine that the world around him was not just concrete and neon and chemicals. After he had sat for a while on a bench kicking the gravel with the cap of his shoe he thought that it really didn't matter if Edith were buried here or somewhere else or if she had been burned and her ashes thrown to the winds. The most important thing was that the psychiatrist and the Helpers where he lived and the psychologists and the educational specialists in the directorate and whoever else was involved should not make him forget her simply by removing all traces of her and manipulating files he himself would never see. Edith was more than a word which would disappear from the language. She was not to be condemned to perpetual oblivion while he was free and could do what he wanted until he finally couldn't take it any more and they would work their will on him.

He suddenly felt in contact with Edith; she whispered to him with the voice of the wind that he must not give up, that he was fighting for their common cause. For a moment she sat next to him so that a tiny, vibrant warmth spread through the half of his body near to her. She told him that she would always be by his side even though he couldn't feel it all the time, and she asked only one thing: not to be forgotten, that she was not to become a casual word which might disappear overnight. Her life had had too much meaning for that even though she had had a hard time seeing it in those final years when everything had gone the way they had feared and she had lost her strength. She reminded him of everything. Of the night they crossed Town Hall Square after having sold everything they owned. Of their happiness, their sense of being reborn. Of the village they found near Nice with its cafes and the communist workers and peasants and Jasper whom she was expecting while he sat bent over his typewriter and wrote the books which gave him peace in his soul. Of the villa they had bought in Frederiksberg where they would have an open house for all their friends once a month. And of how their relationship at that time was inconceivable unless they went to bed together several times a week, either during the afternoon or at night when she would crawl in with him and blow on his neck until he woke up and embraced her, humming with pleasure. All that was not to be forgotten, cancelled out. She mustn't just become a name which he would recall years later, if he survived the treatment and married another girl, and about which he would say: 'Edith? that was the name of a girl I was once married to.'

He got up, left the cemetery and finally realized where he was when he saw the silhouette of the Tuborg breweries between two superblocks. Some time later he was on Strandvej, walking towards the city. He saw nobody anywhere. No cafes were open, the buses were running empty and inside the houses people were turning off their tv sets, pulling the drapes and going to bed. He walked as fast as he could. Svanemøllen, Østerbrogade, Trianglen – he just kept on walking and after a while he began to feel that time didn't exist anymore. It was only when he reached what had once been the Lakes that he slowed down and finally stopped. How long had he been walking without thinking of anything but putting one foot in front of the other, feeling his heart beat, his lungs expand and the nerves in his scalp quiver? For an hour, two hours? He didn't care, not least because while walking he had come to feel twenty years younger and capable of great things again. He felt able to beat down any resistance, avoid any traps which were laid for him and finally to stand in the middle of this parking place in the old Lake where the bird-island had been in his boyhood and shout at the top of his voice so everybody in the buildings around him would wake up: all those who worked in the various government offices and institutes, those with mum-and-dad-cards and those without, the active-women and the passive-women and the old who didn't know what the word old meant anymore because they too had gone to sleep with the notion that they were living in what was called the harmonious age. He wanted to shout so loud that the walls of oblivion would collapse and all the lost words would be remembered again, words like 'imagination', 'dream', 'adventure'. And more than that: the cement under his feet would crack and split and dissolve and he would be on the bird-island again where he used to go when he was a boy, and around him the ducks and swans and gulls would gather in great numbers, and if he dug in the wet steaming earth the worms would appear so he could use them as bait. Spring would have come, finally, and his mother would call out to him from a window in an old red-brick apartment building on the embankment to come and have dinner, so that he and his friends would have to jump quickly into their home-made dinghy and paddle across to the mainland.

But nothing happened. The lights didn't come on in the windows, people didn't get dressed and didn't appear in the street and the cement didn't crack. Not even a policeman showed up to charge him with disorderly conduct. Everything was quiet around him. He saw only a plastic bag which blew past his feet and under a parked car. Then tiredness hit all of a sudden. It entered his temples, pressed his eyeballs like two thumbs, but he knew that his brain wouldn't calm down now, even if he took a taxi home and went to bed. It would go on working with new fantasies which as the night went on would become less and less endurable, and just around dawn they would force him out of bed and over to his desk where the bottle of pills waited to be emptied. Only in the morning would he fall asleep, hoping not to awake before evening. He might as well keep himself up until physical exhaustion reached the point where even the brain would have to give up and he finally collapsed, whether it was on a bench or in a doorway. After he had been standing for a while contemplating the plastic bag he began wandering across the parking place, past the remains of the old bridge across the lake and on towards the center of the city. Now and then he would sit down on the kerb and sleep for some minutes with his head between his knees. Once he fell on his side and slid into a sleeplike state which must have lasted for some time, because it was getting to be morning when he started up eerily hearing Edith screaming somewhere. It was only after a few minutes that he came to and realized that he was not on his way to the desk and the pills. The city was waking up around him, the first people were appearing, the buses were running at shorter and shorter intervals, and something like light began filtering down through the low-hanging clouds. Gradually more people came on the streets and the cars began coming in a thick stream. There they were, all those he had thought he could arouse for one euphoric moment, squeezed in behind the wheel with their hard, grouchy expressions, on their way to work which, they had long forgotten, was without any meaning, even though some reflex at the backs of their minds kept telling them that they were working for the common good. The only people who were smiling in the whole mass of people on the sidewalks and in the cars and buses were the healthy and energetic-looking active-women on the posters that he had helped create. And then the children. Some children here and there on their way to school had time for smiles, for something like laughter, something that seemed like fun – even if it was nothing other than kicking empty cans in the gutter or grabbing hold of traffic signs and running around them a few times. Would anything be different when they grew up? Or would they never have a chance to survive the treatment which they underwent at the hands of the total-school teachers and psychologists? Would they come to believe in a few years that games and fun were relics of a distant past, when the experiences of the individual had lain at the center of things?

At one point he began following four children, two boys and two girls, who turned a corner. He wanted to hear what they were saying to each other. He wanted to know what the elementary joy was they still had, which enabled them to giggle, poke each other and swing their bags in the way children always had. Then he stopped. The hairs rose on his arms, a

79

lump caught in his throat. No, it couldn't be. He was mistaken. It was something he was dreaming. He was exhausted. He was hallucinating. But when the children stopped at a pedestrian crossing and waited for the green light he realized that he wasn't wrong. He went right up to the children.

'Hi,' he said. 'Hi there, Jasper!'

The boy turned to him.

Silence.

'How are you?'

He got no reply. The boy just kept on staring at him and became more and more frightened. And then the image of Jasper in pyjamas and with his hands in front of his face reappeared in his consciousness. It became clearer and clearer as the boy kept on staring at him and stepped out onto the street so that the cars braked screeching and chased him back onto the sidewalk. But a child might be terrified by joy as well, he thought. Jasper might be dumbfounded by the joy of seeing him again. In a moment they would embrace, he would lift up Jasper and they would kiss each other and in a little while he would take Jasper's hand and they would escape – from the city, to the country, where there were still a few forest lakes with trout. But when the light changed to green the boy and the three other children hurried across the street. He ran after them fearing that he would be stopped as a child molester by passers-by because he was unshaven and his clothes dirty and his shoes muddy. But the only ones who tried to stop him touching the boy, when he had caught up with him and took him gently by the arm, were the three other children. He smiled at them and said that he wasn't a strange man like they thought, he was actually Jasper's dad and if they let him talk in peace to him they would hear that he wasn't lying. But he had hardly calmed them down before the boy tore himself away and took three steps backwards so he ended up on the road-way and was chased back by the cars again. And he still looked just as terrified.

'Why did you call me dad a moment ago if you keep on pretending you don't recognize me?' he asked. '*Why*, Jasper?'

The boy shook his head and looked pleadingly at the other three children.

'I don't want to hurt you!' he went on and felt himself running out of words. Was it his dissolute appearance which made Jasper so afraid that he dropped his bag? His beard, his red eyes, his unkempt hair, his wet, grimy clothes and his muddy shoes? Or was it something else? Was it true, after all, that Jasper . . .

The question fell out of his mouth. He wanted to stop it, but was unable to:

'How did mummy die, Jasper? How did mummy die?'

Suddenly tears came to the boy's eyes. He covered his face with his hands and cried so he shook all over. The other three children looked at the boy, at him and at the boy again. Then one of them picked up the bag and whispered something to the boy so he came to himself for a moment. And then all four ran as fast as they could until they turned a corner and left him standing with his exhaustion which was hammering at his temples and pressing his eyeballs again and making him unable to see anything but the image of Jasper in the living-room the night it happened.

Late that morning he finally got home. He walked the rest of the way as in a trance: out through Vesterbro, across Valby hill and out Roskildevej to super-community West. He succeeded in finding the new block where he had been moved. He passed the canteen and the Helpers' office which was fortunately closed and on to the elevator and to the fourteenth floor. There was a notice in the corridor for him saying that he had forgotten to attend the last AC meeting and that a serious talk with him was necessary. He looked at himself in the mirror. He was in even worse shape than he had thought. His eyes weren't just red around the edges, they were bloodshot. His mouth was blackened with dust and dirt and his hair was not just unkempt – it stuck out hysterically in all directions. He forced himself to light a cigarette while he looked at himself in the mirror and kept the smoke in his lungs until he felt dizzy. Are they right? he thought when his knees refused to support him any longer. But he didn't fall over. He folded slowly, rolling onto the floor while the cigarette fell out of his hand and rolled onto the doormat. Are they right? he thought. Are you simply unbalanced?

CHAPTER SEVEN

'Don't forget you have a past as a writer,' they told him. 'That you are, so to speak, a professional of the imagination. Further, it is clear from your novels that you are plagued by guilt-feelings. You alone want to bear the burden of all the world's sins on your shoulders, and you cannot distinguish between the important and the unimportant. You are obsessed with pointless details and violent visions, and you are often the victim of escapist fantasies which can become nightmares. Correct?'

He nodded tiredly and let the Helpers continue their analysis:

'You saw your wife die, on that we can certainly agree. You are probably also right in that you had been having a fight, maybe even a rather violent one; let us say, one which bordered on the fatal. There are times in the lives of everyone when everything breaks down. Love becomes hate, and everyday duties, of the kind that belong, after all, to daily life, seem boring and constraining. Since man is not without faults he must find an outlet for this boredom and this imaginary constriction. And then the ball is rolling. Usually these crises don't last more than a night, and had your wife not died in the hallway you would probably have reconciled your differences the next morning. You had been drinking heavily during the evening – here we also agree with you – and more than dangerously, direct from the bottle. Your wife with good reason fears for your health and runs into the hallway and rings the bell to get us. She stumbles, and then it happens. In her fall her head strikes the wall and later the hard tile floor. You don't react at once. But then you stagger into the hall, see your wife lifeless on the floor, with blood running from her mouth. You throw yourself at her, and try to shake her awake. In the meantime we are on our way. We reach your apartment and enter – and here we make our mistake: we think you are causing your wife's death and we state this in your file – undeniably, supported by your own repeated statements to the effect that you killed her. You told us that not only before we sent you to be pumped out, but also during the following days when you were moving about like a sleepwalker. Therefore we saw no other way out than to send you to the state hospital. It is only after going through the situation again that we realize the truth – which we have just given you. But your imagination keeps on fooling you and connects with your exaggerated feelings of guilt. What might be understandable as sorrow that your wife died following a violent fight with you, becomes instead the conviction that you killed her. And, since then, you have been a captive of your imagination to the extent that you finally collapsed. Had we been only a few minutes late, your cigarette might have set your apartment on fire and caused the entire building to burn down. That's rather a lot to sacrifice to your powers of the imagination!'

He didn't object. In a way it all sounded logical and correct. If he couldn't remember that he had been sent to be pumped out and had been moving around like a sleepwalker for some days before being sent to the state hospital how could he then trust his memory of the evening it happened? Perhaps the truth was somewhere in between. He had beaten Edith so she had run from him, but on the way to the door she had fallen. At first he had not thought it was serious, but when the blood began running from her mouth he had become afraid and had bent over her and shaken her. That was the scene Jasper had witnessed from the living-room and if Jasper was afraid of him it was probably only because he had looked like an exploded scarecrow with his bloodshot eyes, hair sticking out and day-old beard. Or was Jasper the only witness to the truth, the proof that the Helpers were lying? Ought he to try and contact him again now that he knew his route to school, but in a more relaxed way and properly dressed? He didn't pursue the idea further because his brain simply couldn't hold any more questions, and demanded one thing only: complete quiet for a long time. If he wanted to become normal again he would probably do well to listen to the Helpers who were more friendly than they had been for a long time and who perhaps did not have all the nasty ulterior motives he had credited them with for years. They gave him coffee, chocolate and cigarettes and offered to talk with him as often as he wanted, even in the middle of the night. Finally they encouraged him to do something serious about the AC exercises (for his own good), and told him that he would soon receive regular invitations for gatherings with dancing, lotteries and performances which the super-community arranged once a month for people like him – lonely people and others who made life difficult for themselves.

'Are there many of us?' he asked.

'Where there are people, there are problems,' the Helpers replied gently.

He devoted himself to the AC exercises with all his strength. He beat the rag dolls and the foam-rubber monsters. He bawled out the anonymous male figures which were shown to him on slides at an ever-faster rate; he accused them of being malicious, petty, pedantic, tyrannical, stupid, filthy-minded and much else of the same kind. It was as though he finally found release, as though a lot of knots had been suddenly loosened in him. Could the fight with Edith, their argument and even Edith's death have been avoided if she and he had seen the value of the AC exercises to begin with? If *he* had? He took part most eagerly in a hate-run around the superblock. This was something new the aggression psychologists had worked out. At a given time the residents were to meet at the front door of the superblock in track suits and plimsolls. Then they were divided into four teams under the leadership of Helpers who had past experience as sergeants in the army. The Helpers commanded them first to hop up and down in one place and to swing their arms, and then they were commanded to run faster and faster. The Helpers ran alongside them and shouted that they should think of all the people who had bothered them in the past. When they had been running for a while and were perspiring freely, the Helpers excited them to yell in chorus: Shoot them! Murder them! Exterminate them! Some participants declined to shout but were soon gripped by the collective hatred. The shouts echoed between the buildings as the four teams went in four different directions. The shouts came from everywhere as though the entire superblock was put on a war footing and all the residents were convinced that no matter what enemy approached he would be crushed. Shoot! Murder! Exterminate! Some of the participants collapsed from exhaustion, others slowed down, but at no point did the hate lessen in intensity. He kept himself among the front runners and the faster he ran, the louder he yelled, the more sweat dripped from his forehead and the harder the blood throbbed in his temples – the more faces appeared in his mind. Suddenly he recalled a grade-school teacher who had once pinched his cheek so he had a blue mark there for days afterwards, and his hate knew no bounds. Murder him! Then he recalled boyhood playmates who had stolen his toys or smeared jam on his face or tattled to his parents about something he had done. Shoot them! he yelled. Exterminate them! The faces appeared and disappeared one after the other, sometimes fading into one another as in a film; classmates from high school who had teased him because he was no good at soccer; university professors who had refused to see him when he was having problems with his studies; fellow-students who had wanted to write as he had but dared not admit it and who therefore criticized his first stories in the student press as malevolently as they could. An old lady in whose house he had once rented a room and who had refused him access to the toilet; youth rebels from the sixties who had charged him with not being revolutionary enough; writers and critics he had fought in the papers; the psychiatrist at the state hospital; the BLIMP section chiefs; the bejewelled lady behind the counter in the directorate for the issue and withdrawal of mum-and-dad-cards; they were all to be shot, murdered, exterminated. He almost admitted to himself that he felt happy as he was running around past the blocks of buildings yelling and sweating in time with the others.

After a sauna and a shower there came an hour of self-criticism for him, together with the Helpers. Most were sent home with the information that they would be seen during the following weeks, but the five who had yelled the loudest were accommodated at once, and he was the first of those five. He was relaxed, the blood was pulsing in his veins, he drew his breath deeply and quietly. He could clearly see that he felt abnormally persecuted as so many people were after him and had been since he was little – he could remember them all. Now that the knots had been loosened in him for a while he felt no need to object when the Helpers suggested that he was unusually self-centered and obviously had been in his division of the world into friends and enemies. The former were those he felt secure with, those who didn't disagree with him, and the latter (who had clearly become an entire army as the years had passed) were those with whom he felt insecure at the least provocation. It was as though the world thought only of him, as though other people only existed as extensions of his ego-experience. Didn't the teacher in grade-school, his playmates and later his schoolmates, his fellow-students with their dreams of writing and the professors and the old ladies whose rooms he rented and the psychiatrist at the state hospital and the people at the directorate who issued and withdrew the mum-and-dad-cards have nothing else to think about except

87

this one thing: to drive him mad? Couldn't he even have a conversation with other people without relating it to his own ego? Wasn't he ever able to *listen*? And wasn't it this same exaggerated self-reliance which was then transformed into an equally exaggerated sense of guilt, as though the Lord had chosen him to bear the sins of the world on his shoulders, to be the suffering exception to humanity?

He agreed with them in everything, also in that being a writer for him was not at all a matter of communicating something significant to the reader but merely an attempt at compensating, at pulling himself up by his bootstraps, pointing at himself and saying: See how big I am! See how well I write! When would he ever discover that the world was not just him on one side and everyone else on the other?

Would he discover it now, during the next week or so? He started to greet his neighbors, tried to talk to the children playing among the parked cars, addressed the lady in the canteen when he ordered food and not as he did usually with his attention deliberately focussed on a newspaper or something on a nearby table. He listened to the tv discussions without getting angry at the participants, and thought about what they said, letting their opinions sink into him. He even bought a pile of socially oriented novels, avoided writing 'ha! ha!' in the margin when they were exceptionally incompetent. Instead he read them as an ordinary reader would who followed the characters from page to page, took an exclamation point as an exclamation point, became depressed when the characters became depressed at the everyday treadmill and happy when they finally achieved a new faith in existence with work for the Common Good, their Sunday excursions to the last protected areas, progressive tv serials and prizes for the prettiest bonsai trees. He convinced himself that the adventure was not really over or that it was only to be found on other continents or planets. Perhaps it was really all around him and populated by thousands of people who found meaning in existence in what was close by and in their work. Perhaps the socially oriented novels were simply the adventures of the present, tales about people who suddenly stopped, packed their bags so to speak, made the inner journey (instead of running away to places where happiness wasn't to be found anyway) and finally reached the sunrise; the meaning behind it all. His arrogance had made him blind, his self-centeredness had cut him off from his surroundings, his conceitedness had made him look down on other people and his escapism had made him despise the adventures of everyday life.

He decided to attend the first Saturday meeting arranged by the supercommunity for people like him. It was held in an athletic hall not many blocks from where he lived. The place was already crowded when he got there and sat down at a table near the entrance. A band was playing in a corner and people were dancing. Before he realized it, he too, was on the dance floor, after a lady had come up to him, taken him by the wrist and dragged him off. She was about fifty, and had the dead stub of a cheroot bobbing up and down between her lips. Didn't he think the band was good? she asked. Didn't he think that it was a great idea generally, having a night like this once a month? He nodded. Was he divorced? He kept on nodding for fear that she would drown him in sympathy if he told her that he was a widower. The woman seemed unattractive in every way and he caught himself wanting to flick the stub of her cheroot across the room. But wouldn't that merely indicate that he still hadn't shed his arrogance? Wasn't the woman who was holding him tighter and tighter and who shortly would lay her cheek against his, simply an ordinary person like most other people? People he had kept away from for decades and hardly thought about while he was writing his self-centered novels? The women and the men around him with their haggard faces, their hair-nets and flowery dresses, suits and hearing-aids, polished shoes and their hopes for a few hours of pathetic entertainment – weren't they simply as people had always been? And wasn't he one of them? What gave him the right to be annoyed by the stub of a cheroot? Perhaps one or

89

more details in his own appearance might be irritating her just as much: his nose, his sideburns which were probably unevenly cut, his small ears? Hadn't the woman just as much a right to think she was exceptional as he had?

When the music stopped the woman pulled him after her to his table. He didn't want to isolate himself, he wanted to be as the others, and soon he was involved in conversations with the lady and her friends about everything between heaven and earth. As he was the only man at the table he gradually became the center of attention while the packs of cheroots circulated, the cakes were devoured in enormous numbers and the coffee poured constantly from the pots. All the women at the table were middle-aged active-women and they all expatiated on the problems that they had because, while it was important that they were working in government departments they all missed being able to just 'be about the house' as they had done before. They had problems with their husbands. They drank. They had difficulty sleeping. Later they stopped talking about themselves and instead talked about the other men and women who were present. The gossip raised their spirits as they pointed around the room. There was the man who had refused for ten years to go to bed with his wife. There was the woman who couldn't leave young men alone. There was the one who shoplifted in the supermarket and who was therefore always searched at the checkout. And there was the one who had received both the grey and the blue slip and would soon receive the red one which meant that her children would be taken from her. He looked curiously at this one. She was sitting by herself and snapped at anyone who asked her to dance. Once she spat at the dancers so that the Helpers, who were gathered in a crowd at the entrance, came over and admonished her. She was thin, wearing a sad, grey dress, her hair was greasy and her glasses made her eyes look abnormally large. When she kept on snarling and finally began throwing empty beer-bottles between the feet of those who were dancing, two Helpers lifted her up and carried her outside.

For some reason he couldn't stop thinking about her for the

rest of the evening while he did what he could to seem interested, laughed when the ladies told jokes, looked sad when they told a sad story, danced with all of them and drank all the coffee they poured in his cup. After the gathering ended at midnight he accompanied the ladies for a while and promised to come and play bridge with them one Sunday soon and maybe put their husbands in a better mood. But the only one he wanted to go and see was the one the Helpers had carried out. Not because he felt he had anything in common with her, he thought – and immediately corrected himself for thinking that sort of arrogant thought which precluded her maybe not having anything in common with him. He thought of her as he fell asleep, and she was on his mind the next morning as he awoke and went into the kitchen to put on the water for coffee, looking out the window at the parking place as he did so. Was this a coincidence looking like something deliberate? Was he seeing visions? Out of the block opposite came the police, dragging three children screaming, kicking and crying as they were put into a minibus. When the woman with the glasses and the greasy hair came out shortly afterwards and began running after the minibus he forgot coffee and breakfast, hurried into the bedroom, put on his shirt and pants and ran out of the apartment and down all the steps because he didn't want to wait for the elevator. When he came out he saw four Helpers coming around a corner while the minibus disappeared in the opposite direction. The Helpers approached the woman who was now on all fours beating her fists bloody against the pavement. He went up to her. She looked up at him:

'Help me!' she cried.

He didn't answer.

'Help me!' she repeated.

Then the Helpers arrived. They lifted her up. She kicked her legs in the air, shook her head and turned around to face him:

'Wag-tail!' she yelled. 'You're a wag-tail! Just like all the others!'

He didn't know how long he remained standing there, staring after her as she was carried into the building. The air was still cold, as though spring had finally decided never to come. It began to rain with a fine, dustlike rain and a supersonic airplane made all the windowpanes rattle and a tv aerial on a roof snap and slide past the drainpipe and fall in pieces onto the hood of a car. In the meantime the Helpers had come back and he heard himself asking them what was the matter with the woman that her children had to be taken away. The wind carried their answer to him so that it came to his ears in snatches and made him see what sort of a change had been happening to him. But now he had recovered from the total exhaustion which left him open to the treatment; and he could once again see how things hung together. He was rested as he had not been for a long, long time, and the reply of the Helpers called forth a mighty rage in him. It was almost as though they were the very words he had been waiting for:

'It isn't easy to create the New Man.'

The answer kept circling in the air, struck a building and bounced off to strike another building and then back again, echoing with ever increasing force. Like a whirlwind it roared among the parked cars, was sucked in under them and thrown out the other side, it became a new whirlwind and was again bounced back and forth between the buildings. The New Man! He didn't know what to do with his newly-found energy. He felt he could push the buildings and they would collapse like cards, that he could pick up the cars and throw them through the air, scrape the sky clean of dirty clouds and ignite the sun so it would hit the area like an explosion. And in the middle of all this he heard Edith again somewhere. Perhaps she was standing behind a car, or hiding behind a fence. She gave him new courage not to give up, to keep on fighting for their common cause, and when he replied that he would not give up he felt warmth stream through his body as though she had come out of hiding and had touched him. And then he ran as fast as he could after the Helpers and danced around them like a schoolboy, shouting:

'I'm a killer, killer, killer . . .'

Was it Edith who gave him the idea or did he think of it

himself? At any rate, he shouted as loudly as he could that if they wouldn't believe him he saw no way out other than proving that he was right. They would never succeed in changing him, he was and would remain a murderer, and only on the day that they admitted it and declared him guilty would he stop killing other people. Other people? they asked, appalled, and he confirmed it: yes, other people, perhaps his neighbors, some of the ladies he had danced with, people in the street, in government offices, the cafeteria waitresses in the superblock, maybe some foreign workers; he would murder them all, shoot them, exterminate them. He had already decided on the first victim, he yelled, but they wouldn't know who it was until they saw the body. If they wanted to catch him they had better start following him now. They continued to look blankly at him. He took some steps backwards while he heard Edith continue to encourage him as his legs carried him towards the exit. He felt in his pocket and discovered that he had fifty crowns, enough for a cab. Behind him he heard the Helpers shouting that he must stop at once, but he just laughed at them, laughed so loudly that people turned to stare at him, and just as the Helpers came rushing up to him he jumped into a cab and ordered the driver to go to Dragør as fast as possible. He turned around and saw through the rear window how the Helpers ran out of breath and looked around for a cab so they could follow him. But none came. Edith had managed everything down to the last detail, of course, so that nothing would go wrong.

'Hello, Bridgit!'

She looked at him, not surprised at all.

'I knew you would come back,' she said and, puffing at a cigarette, let him in.

She was entertaining a man his own age, and they were enjoying their Sunday lunch.

'This is my brother Villy,' she said.

'Torben,' he said, extending his hand.

'Are you hungry?' she asked.

'A little,' he replied and wondered how long her brother was staying. Maybe he was from the provinces and would be staying with her for a fortnight.

'Are you from Copenhagen?' he asked, sitting down on a chair the girl provided.

'You might say so,' the brother answered. 'I'm a journalist with the tv.'

'Villy is working on a new program to be called "The People Complain",' the girl said. 'It's a program where all who want to can air their grievances if they have been treated badly.'

He looked at the girl and felt how he lost his energy all of a sudden. He felt completely out of place, sitting at their lunch table dressed only in shoes, shirt and pants. At the same time he felt as though Edith was no longer at his side, and without her he would not have the strength to kill the girl when he was alone with her. And to make it all even more difficult the girl began to talk about him. About how he had been working in BLIMP but had got tired of it all and that she had, so to speak, picked him up in the canteen at the bureau where he was sitting with a cup of strong tea and about how she had then brought him here where he had slept and slept only to awake and ramble on about how he had caused his wife's death. 'Isn't it true?' she asked, looking at him. 'Isn't it true that you went around thinking that it was you who had killed her?'

'It's not just something I believed,' he answered and couldn't understand why Edith wasn't close by him anymore.

'Do you mean to say that you actually killed her?' the brother said, curious, and patted a flowery handkerchief he had in his breast pocket. 'That you weren't simply being dictated to by the circumstances?'

'Yes ...'

'And they refuse to recognize that you are guilty of this ... killing. And that is all you want: to be told that you are guilty? So you are fighting a long and hard fight with the result that they simply got tired of you and try to convince you that your wife died ... by accident?'

94

'How did you guess?' he asked.

'I'm a journalist.'

He became attentive again and before long he had told the whole story to the girl's brother.

'It couldn't be better,' the brother said. 'You are a gift from heaven ... exactly the person I need for my first program!'

Were there still people who hadn't given up? Who refused to let themselves be throttled by the system? Were there still people fighting for the truth to be known? He looked at the girl's brother and only now realized how sympathetic he seemed. He was well-dressed, but not dandified. His eyes were conscientious and his face had something earnest, something searching about it. They agreed that he would move in with him so he could be in peace from the Helpers and avoid more treatment. Then they would plan how to do it, and next Saturday, when the first installment of 'The People Complain' was shown, he would be smuggled in the back door to the studio and put face to face with the camera so he could speak his case to the entire population.

He felt happy. He felt more than happy: he felt blissful – and not least because he felt that Edith was once more at his side and she was supporting him in his trust that here was an all-time chance to carry their common fight through to victory.

CHAPTER EIGHT

The journalist lived in a modernized farmhouse south of Copenhagen. He had built a wall around it so he could be safe from intruders, enjoying in quiet his spice herbs, his rare trees which he had brought back from his trips to Asia and Latin America, his Italian terrace with its tiles and Etruscan vases and barbecue, his antiques and old books and countless games. For ten years he had been building his little paradise, he said. Here he could be at peace, here he could find strength to live and work.

They played darts. They played chess. They played cards and Chinese checkers and any number of other games. Mostly the journalist won, but after a few days he began to catch up because his thoughts were falling into place. Finally he succeeded in winning two games of chess in a row, which convinced him that if only he could be just as calm and collected when he went on tv he would be able to elicit the most phenomenal reactions. He was not, after all, able to kill in cold blood, and he realized that it hadn't been Edith's intention for him to do so. She had simply suggested that he visit the girl in Dragør so that he could meet her brother and then go and stay with him so that they might plan together how he was to put his case to the entire people of Denmark. The many games were a form of training in self-control: it was vitally important that he would not get tangled in contradictions in front of the camera. He must be himself, but at the same time play a role, and play it to perfection.

The journalist turned out to be a good cook as well. He had lots of French, Italian, Jewish and Latin American cookbooks, and even though the ingredients he obtained at the nearest supermarket weren't exactly first class he still succeeded in producing exciting dishes. His kitchen was painfully neat; the stove had been specially designed for him with a gas range and range hood of wrought iron; herbs and spices were hanging from the ceiling in long rows: thyme, lovage, fennel. On a shelf he saw vinegar, oil and six different kinds of mustard, and all the pots and pans were of copper lined with tin. While dinner was preparing they had vintage sherry, with dinner they had red wine which the journalist had brought back from his travels, and with coffee they had framboise in iced snifters. When they weren't talking about the tv program their conversation ranged over many things. It turned out that the journalist had been married once, but he wasn't told why he had got divorced – just that he felt happiest being single: then he was in control of things, nothing disturbed him or crossed his wishes, and he was free of all the problems with the mum-and-dad-cards which made life hell for many of his colleagues. Since he had no children he wasn't plagued by the deep fear that they would be taken from him. He laughed and added that maybe he was building on a dream. Perhaps he had constructed a castle in the air for himself, but wasn't a castle in the air better at any rate than what one saw nowadays? And as yet there were no plans for taking a superhighway through his bedroom and only in about ten years would the superblocks start eating up the little municipality to which he belonged. They also talked about books. The journalist knew that he had once written novels, but he didn't really care much for them, he apologized, his hand on his heart. Not that he preferred the socially oriented novels, those he despised profoundly. But because he only enjoyed the sort of literature which gave him esthetic pleasure. He read Proust, *The Compleat Angler*, old English travellers' tales and, as for Danish literature, Jacob Paludan and Knud Sønderby and Frank Jaeger. Good literature was like good port, to be enjoyed in small doses, with a fire blazing in the fireplace. It must not, for anything in the world, disturb one's conscience or stir up an enormous expressionistic register of emotions. He felt the same way about music. He had never got further than Mozart.

He wondered where the journalist found the strength. It took strength, surely, to establish oneself as he had done and disengage one hundred per cent when one crossed one's own threshold. He had always envied people like that, people who weren't sloppy and who found the meaning of life in an essay by Paludan, some Mozart and a meal garnished with thyme and lovage. Each time he himself had tried something of the kind, it had gone wrong. Either he lost patience because he lacked the extra energy and drive, or a thousand and one things came up and made him so nervous that he would overturn the window-box with its herbs or spill coffee on the books he had had expensively bound. Or he would be unable to let the bottle of port alone, but had to drink it all in an hour or two so that he would be even more confused than he was to begin with; smoking even more cigarettes and looking for more to drink, only to collapse in bed and wake up next morning with a thundering headache, perspiring all over, plagued by nightmares. He was in everything the exact opposite of a true bon vivant. How were bon vivants constructed? Didn't the journalist ever feel the urge to destroy everything around him? And how did his entire lifestyle harmonize with his interest in helping him to go on tv? Couldn't he lose his position if everything went as they planned and he turned Denmark upside down by telling how he had murdered Edith and how they had later denied that he was guilty and finally that he had even done it?

'Once in a while one has to admit that there is such a thing as one's conscience,' the journalist said, 'and even I, after all, have an urge to become involved in meaningful work.'

He leaned back in his broad-backed wicker chair and fondled his cat, which had jumped up on his lap. He spoke slowly and carefully – a bit too carefully, perhaps: it was as though the word conscience in his mouth simply became another kind of spicy herb, something rather like the raspberry brandy he was sipping with his nose in the snifter. Shortly after he put his legs on a stool and looked out the window as though he were waiting for the sun to come and get the plants and rare trees in the garden growing, warm up the Italian terrace and make it possible to cook dinner on the barbecue. For a while they said nothing to one another. Then the journalist looked at his watch and announced that he was going to retire; he never went to bed on 'the wrong side of midnight'; if he didn't get ten hours of sleep he wouldn't be able to work. But he was welcome to remain alone in the room and warm himself at the fire. The journalist put the cat in its basket, took Mozart off the turntable and put the bottle with the framboise in front of him if he wanted another glass. He could read what books he pleased, if he promised not to split the spine or leave dirty fingermarks in the margin.

After the journalist had gone to bed he tried to read. An English collection of essays about the joys of simple things. The joy of lighting one's pipe and watching the blue smoke curl into the air. The joy of lying in a haystack and imagining figures in the cloud formations as they went drifting by. The joy of collecting old Indian china. But he couldn't concentrate, couldn't calm down among all the antique furniture, the old pharmacist's bowls, the Danish paintings from the Golden Age, the fire crackling in the fireplace and the cat in its basket aiming blows with its paw at a spider. He still couldn't make it all fit with the journalist's involvement with a tv program which might lead to his being fired. But Edith must know better, he said to himself. And after he had succeeded in getting through an essay about the joy of restoring old cars he went to bed in the guest-room.

* * *

Already, as they were driving towards Copenhagen late Saturday afternoon he began missing the journalist's farmhouse. The week which had passed had already assumed an unreal, almost dreamlike flavor. Reality was back now, as far as he could see, with superblocks, lines of cars, incinerator plants, electric plants and chemical factories. After an hour they had reached the center of the city which it took them another hour to get through. Then they reached Broadcasting House and parked. They avoided the main entrance and thus the guards ('just to be safe', the journalist said), went down the long corridors, past the canteen where he could distinguish many of the social scientists and psychologists whose murderously unimaginative, imagination-killing programs he had hated for ten years, and on to the studio building. They came to studio one. An enormous sign saying 'The People Complain' was the first thing he noticed. It hung by two ropes from the ceiling and was evidently to be lowered just before the program began. An artificial wall divided the studio across the middle, and he wondered if it was to save money. Perhaps they are arranging a social drama on the other side of the wall. It would be an hour before the program started, and the journalist asked him to sit down on a stool in a corner of the studio while he himself saw to it that everything was in order, that the technicians were on their way and refreshments had been ordered for the participants.

'The participants?' he asked.

'Yes, both of us, and then all the people who see to it that we go on the screen,' the journalist answered and hurried up on a platform with two chairs. He placed them at the right distance from one another and ordered the sign saying 'The People Complain' to be lowered right behind them. It was immediately lowered little by little. At one point the journalist cried stop, and then checked the position of the chairs again, and hurried over to some cameramen who had just arrived. He was probably discussing angles and projections with them, he thought, and noticed how popular the journalist seemed. The technicians were constantly offering him beer and cigarettes

100

which he politely declined, and the men were for ever patting each other on the shoulder.

Why had he never noticed the journalist before on tv anyway, he wondered? Had he been transferred from the radio division? Or had he been working off-screen, so that this would be his first program actually on the air, and was that why he was so eager? He gave up trying to figure out the true reason and looked instead at the clock above the door and realized that the time was almost up. The journalist disappeared behind the artificial wall, came back and ordered that the cameras should be shifted slightly and that one of them for some reason should face the wall. And then he signalled that he should come up on the platform with the two chairs. They sat down across one another and for the last time they ran through the procedure they had agreed upon. First, the journalist would say a few words, then it was his turn to present his case, and finally the journalist would ask him for some details. Five minutes left until the cameras rolled. Four, three two. Then the technicians gave the go signal, the journalist crossed his legs, unfolded a sheet of paper and stated the purpose of the program 'The People Complain'. Everyone could bring his or her problems to the program, he said, they would all be taken seriously. Anyone who felt mistreated by society could present his case, although the limited time at his disposal would mean that not all complaints could be considered. He stopped briefly, adjusted his breast-pocket handkerchief and cleared his throat. Then he went on:

'Our first guest tonight has a problem which may seem special. But we have chosen to begin with him precisely to show you how wide-ranging our program will be!'

The journalist introduced him and went on, smiling:

'But perhaps you had better tell us in your own words what your complaint is?'

He felt his stomach heave, his hands break out in sweat, his mouth go dry and his ears ring: all the familiar symptoms of camera-fright from the times when he was interviewed about his novels or participated in one round-table discussion after

another. Was he in the same studio? Were some of the technicians even the same people as then? He sensed the cameras
zooming in on him and he felt momentarily like doing what he
had done once during a round-table discussion on ecology and
announcing that he did not feel well. But then he thought of
Edith. He couldn't let her down; this was not just for his own
sake. It was for their relationship and love that he was fighting
and hence for the right of everybody to be happy and to stay
together. And he was fighting for Jasper, for the new and
better world which he and his schoolmates should have. He
held his breath and counted to ten. Then he became calm. He
knew he could deal with the situation:

'I have killed my wife,' he said.

He paused and looked directly at the camera. When he
began talking again, he felt how the words came of themselves. He did not get excited, he did not dramatize the tale but
calmly reported his story. He talked about how happy their
marriage had been in the beginning, about their sojourns in
the south of France, about the books he wrote and the films
Edith enthusiastically edited when they got back (he knew that
it was having an effect on the viewers when he mentioned her
by name), about the house in Frederiksberg and Jasper's early
years. He talked about their living beyond their means following his first two successful novels, about how their finances
began to look bad and how they had to sell the villa and move
to a superblock and he had to find work at BLIMP. He talked
about the changes in society, the new serfdom made up of
ever-increasing taxes and rents and compulsory insurance,
about concrete and boredom and state tutelage and AC and the
law requiring obligatory tests for all who wanted children – all
the things which had gradually made it impossible to live in a
happy marriage. Gradually he could not longer channel his
aggressions in the right direction, they were only expressed
within the four walls of his home, and soon he was blaming
Edith for everything. As though she had been behind the law
of mandatory tests for those who wanted children, as though
she had wanted to rewrite Hans Christian Andersen and pro-

hibit all non-socially oriented literature, as though she were administering the supercommunities, building the super-blocks, hiring thousands and thousands of Helpers and giving them keys so they could enter people's apartments when they wanted, as though she were tightening the bonds of serfdom and making a life of freedom impossible, setting the so-called Common Good above the happiness of the individual and striking down those who deviated in the least from the accept-able norms. And then the night it happened – he couldn't take it any more. He had been drinking like a fish. Then he had gone crazy because Edith for once refused to join in his fury. He hadn't just hit her. He had beaten her through and through. And not only had he beaten her head against the wall so she lost consciousness. He had also beaten it against the tile floor in the hallway when she was already dead and the blood was trickling from her mouth. In other words, it was the very opposite of an accident ...

'I think I should break in here,' the journalist said.

'By all means,' he answered, as they had agreed he would.

'You said: an accident?'

'It is not recognized that I killed my wife,' he said. 'It is assumed that it was an accident ... that she fell and hit her head ...'

'Who supposes that?'

'The Helpers where I live, the psychiatrists, the directorate for the issue and withdrawal of mum-and-dad-cards ... in short, everybody denies that I am guilty.'

'Even so, your son has been taken from you?'

'Correct.'

'For what reason?'

'Because I am unbalanced.'

Never had he felt in better balance. He caught a glimpse of himself on a tv screen some feet away and saw that he was not nervous-looking, and contrary to the agreement with the journalist (that he would be questioned for at least five minutes), he began talking directly to the camera again. He knew that this was the chance to talk to the viewers as no one had talked to them in years. He could talk about all the things they had forgotten long ago; about being a human being, and not just a tiny piece in a gigantic, distant plan which no one knew anything about – not even the ones who thought they knew. He felt Edith at his side again and the side of his body which was turned towards her became warm right from his shoulder to his ankle. And he knew that Jasper was sitting right now on the floor in the apartment belonging to his step-parents and looking at him and maybe suddenly, for the first time, feeling proud of having him as his daddy. Everywhere he was being listened to, he felt, and continued to talk about the words he had helped eliminate from the language but which now were again to mean something; the word 'love', the word 'responsibility', the word 'devotion', the word 'feeling', the word 'humanity', the word 'honesty', the word 'forgiveness', and the word 'guilt'. He was guilty. He had not been dictated to by 'circumstances' when he killed Edith. But he didn't want some old-fashioned form of punishment, he just wanted one thing: to be told that he knew what he was doing that night even though he was befogged by whiskey. And if he were driven by circumstances then those circumstances were a society which refused to listen to anything *except* circumstances; which denied that each individual had a right to his life and his dream and his untouchable identity. He became warmer and warmer and could sense how people throughout the country were looking at one another wonderingly and also at first afraid because the memory of something lost suddenly made itself felt. But soon they would be gripped by enthusiasm and gather on the streets and in the market-places and light fires, young and old people together. The Helpers would be there too and would give up their belief that they knew what the right thing for everyone was. The politicians and the members of government would be there too because they, like all the others had been caught in a net of lies and unreality. And in a short time everybody would start building a more beautiful and better and humane society, and thousands of laws and rules would be declared invalid.

Nobody would object because nobody would be able to remember who was actually responsible for them, and the books which were hidden away in the library cellars would be brought out again and the socially oriented novels would be used for fuel or burned on huge bonfires at midsummer. The movie houses and the theaters would reopen, and the artists would dare to be artists again and would describe man from all angles and in all aspects; fearful man, demonic man, aggressive and doomed man, but also dancing, loving, dreaming and adventurous and affectionate man. There would be experiments with new lifestyles, new friendly houses full of light with huge gardens near squares with cafes and fountains which would replace the superblocks that wouldn't be too hard to tear down. The superhighways would become superfluous and the grass would sprout through the cracks in the cement; beautiful trains in many colors would roll across the country (but respecting nature and not fouling it up), on rails which would reflect the sunlight. Many small new schools would replace the total-school barracks, schools where the kids would be able to play as much as they wanted but would also learn about the history of mankind, about the great poets and thinkers and composers, about the culture and the past without which there could be no future. Even here in the studio everything would be different. Maybe it *was* already changing, he thought when the journalist got up and ran across the floor and the artificial wall suddenly disappeared and a new platform appeared. The Helpers from where he lived and the psychiatrist from the state hospital and the director from the directorate for the issue and withdrawal of mum-and-dad-cards and shortly after them Jasper all came in and sat down on it. They all smiled at him, except Jasper who was probably just feeling timid about the whole situation, smiling happily over what he had told them, and soon they would join the dance, and everybody else in the tv building would come as well and dance and be happy that they were going to build a better world.

Or were they not smiling out of happiness? Were they

smiling condescendingly at him? Was something happening which would change what should have been a feast into a nightmare? Was he lying at home in his one-room apartment dreaming and knowing that he was dreaming and fighting a desperate fight to wake up and go and get one of the pills which would calm him down? His eyes swam as he saw, on the tv screen, the journalist saying that every accusation required a defense and that the other side would now be heard – all those who had denied that he had killed his wife. The journalist then crossed his legs and leaned forward on the screen as well as on the platform and asked two of the Helpers about it. They immediately declared that they could produce a witness to the effect that it was an accident and not a murder. And then Jasper's face filled the screen. A serious Jasper, a Jasper who looked as though he had become twenty years older, as in a nightmare. And what could he say about it? the journalist asked. What had he seen? Jasper slowly recounted how he had heard his father and mother fight and how it sounded like they were throwing things at each other. Then he had got out of bed and seen his mother fall and soon after lie lifeless on the floor in the hall; and his father had then come and tried to shake her to bring her back to life. That was what he had seen, and it had been so terrible that he had covered his face with his hands and had not noticed anything more before a Helper came to him and gave him a piece of chocolate and followed him to bed and sat by his side for the rest of the night. What could he say about his father? the journalist asked. He could tell that his dad had once been the perfect daddy, but that was many years ago, when he was small and before he went to school. Later it was as though his father refused to have anything to do with him, as though he simply walked around absorbed in his own thoughts and yelling and snarling if he were disturbed. Soon not a day would pass without his father and mother fighting about the smallest things so that he often preferred to lock himself in his room and put cotton in his ears. The director from the directorate for the issue and withdrawal of mum-and-dad-cards broke in and asked if he didn't

106

feel much better in his new home. Yes, now he was much better, he said, just as seriously.

'You're lying, Jasper!' he yelled at the tv screen and then at him. 'You're *lying*!'

A technician or assistant producer or whatever he was came over and said that if he did not restrain himself they would have to remove him. He badly wanted to push him aside and run over to the other platform. He wanted to push them all so they fell over except Jasper whom he would grab and run away with, no matter where, just somewhere where they could talk in peace and he could find out what they had done to him to make him lie. But when it came to the crunch he barely had enough energy to stay where he was and watch the tv screen. By means of photographs from the old apartment and drawings and tables and much else the Helpers tried to prove that he hadn't killed Edith. Then they went on with a discussion of why he nevertheless believed that he had caused her death. And now everybody spoke at the same time. The psychiatrist talked about feelings of guilt as a complex matter, which could, however, be considered a relic of a past which exalted individualism; and the exaggerated belief in the 'personality' as something inviolable. The Helpers agreed and saw in his example a case of how this personality cult might lead to the perfectly antisocial person with all the characteristics of the antisocial person: escapist fantasies, manic self-centeredness, confusion of dream and reality and a belief that life is a personal adventure. New drawings came on the screen, drawings of a man with a circle of barbed wire around him, and drawings of people with lines connecting them to other people; columns of figures were juxtaposed, statistics replaced more statistics and experiments with mice were cited, all of it to show that there was still a way to go before the New Man was created to fit the new, hyper-complex society. But none of the participants in the discussion had any doubt that they would succeed in creating this New Man, and that it would be possible to derive significant scientific information from this case of imaginary guilt, which sprang from a still-living, irrational belief that there was something called 'the core of the personality'.

Finally the journalist came back to him and asked if he had anything to say in his defense. The journalist again seemed relaxed, obviously satisfied with the success of his program.

'You have two minutes at your disposal,' the journalist said and flicked a speck of dust from his jacket sleeve.

He didn't reply. His head ached, and he had difficulty in breathing normally while he tried to figure out why Edith had suddenly deserted him, had rejected him as if he were a creature she didn't want.

CHAPTER NINE

He knew that he had been born three years after the end of
World War Two. He knew what his name was, who his parents were, where he had gone to school, when he had gone to
university, why he had left it, when he had married Edith,
when Jasper had been born and when he had written and
published his two novels. He could write it all down on a piece
of paper with the years and sometimes the day and month
added. There was no doubt about any of this, but maybe they
would want to prove that he had been born earlier or later, that
he had attended entirely different schools than the ones he
wrote down, that he hadn't gone to university at all and had
not been married to Edith or was Jasper's father? And if he
showed them the two novels he had written and pointed to his
name on the cover, they might answer that it was easy enough
to claim that it was his name; he might as well bring them *War
and Peace* and claim that he had written it. When would they
deny that he was who he was and give him a new personality,
provide him with a new name, a different past? He had no
doubt that they were aiming for that, but they wouldn't succeed. He would prepare like mad for their next offensive, and
therefore he decided to remember everything that had ever
happened in his life, down to the last detail. And write it
down. Point by point. Even if it took thousands of pages.

He divided his life into four parts. There were the years from
when he was born and until he was ten. There were the years
from ten to twenty, the last years of grade school, the years of
intermediate school and high school and the first years at
university. Then came the five years when he jumped from
one field to another, got a grant to go to Italy but used it to go to
Paris and study Sartre and eat strawberry tarts with crème
fraiche, returned and got more and more involved in politics,
wrote his first stories, met Edith, joined in the youth rebellion
and claimed power to the imagination, married Edith and
finally got stalled in the rebellion just as she did because
anything *but* imagination came to power. And then he had got
to part four, which he would save to the last – that was the part
the Helpers would most easily be able to challenge because it
involved the developments they were responsible for. Of the
four parts he chose to begin with part two.

Ten years old. He had gone to Langelinie, the harbor where
the little mermaid gazed, to watch visiting American battle-
ships, and they had been given lots of chewing-gum and
chocolate by the sailors. When they had eaten it all they put
modeling clay in the packages and sold them to a boy they met
on the way home. When the boy discovered that he had been
cheated he began to cry, but they just laughed at him and said
that only stupid boys let themselves be cheated. Ten years. His
father had just become a department head in the ministry of
education; his mother's illness had begun to mark her seriously and he had to run constantly to the drugstore and promise to
be back as quickly as possible with the medicine. But sometimes he only got back hours later because he wanted to look at
model ships on the artificial lake which a man controlled by
radio from the land – there were British cruisers and marine
vessels with French flags and tiny motorboats. What more
could he recall from his eleventh year? There was the shoemaker's son whom he hit on the head with a piece of coal
because his big brother was known to have helped the Ger-
mans and had been fetched one day and put on a truck and
spat on by everybody in the neighborhood. He recalled clearly

how he had met the shoemaker's son. It was in the middle of the winter and it had snowed so hard that cars couldn't move and the streetcars barely crawled along. On a corner a truck full of coal had overturned, and he had caught him there stealing coal, and then he had taken a piece and banged him on the head with it, remarking that fuel was for those who hadn't helped the Nazis. He also remembered a teacher they had at school for six months until she left because they teased her about her wig and jumped up and tore it off so she was as bald as the baldest man. He remembered the fragrance of his grandmother's apartment. A fragrance of rose-leaves, preserves and mothballs. Eleven years. He took the intermediate school test and passed, but not as well as his mother and father had hoped with the result that he did not get into the high school they had applied for in the neighborhood but one out in the suburbs. Twelve years. His grandmother died, and for a while the family talked about how she had thrown the priest out of her sick-room two days before with a furious remark to the effect that she had been an atheist all her life and intended to be one still when they carried her out feet first. That episode saddened his mother and she often returned to it during the three years which were left before it was her turn to die in the middle of the afternoon, in the middle of the summer, in a corner of the small plot belonging to their summer-house in North Zeeland.

He remembered the funeral which took place in a small village church near the summer-house, and the days following it when the house became strange and empty so that dad and he decided to go back to Copenhagen even though it would be a month until school started. Copenhagen at the end of July and in early August. No playmates, nothing to do, rain one day and stifling heat the next. If he wanted to go see a film it was bound to be x-rated so that he had to stand outside the movie houses and vainly try to sell his ticket when he had been denied admittance. He had just turned fifteen. Pimples all over his face. The girls wouldn't have anything to do with him, neither the ones his age or the slightly older ones. They

111

wanted to go dancing in Tivoli with the boys who had money, had begun to shave and who weren't afraid of the ticket checkers. In the evening he listened to the American Forces Network on the bakelite radio. He wavered between missing his mother violently and dreaming of being where things happened. Jazz! Jazz concerts, jazz clubs and nightclubs where he would know all the names of all the songs when the girl he was dancing with asked him. Chewing-gum and cigarettes and his first record collection which he got from a second-hand dealer on Ryesgade. And his first girlie magazines which he carefully hid under his mattress so his father wouldn't find them. On the other hand he found *Lady Chatterley's Lover* in his study. He remembered everything. And then the school-year began, and suddenly there were no limits to what he knew about films, jazz and women. He helped start the school's jazz club and already by the time the fall break came he had arranged the first jazz concert in the gymnasium. He set the pace, taught the others in his class how to inhale and showed them all his girlie magazines and the two pages in *Lady Chatterley's Lover* to which the book always opened when he let it fall to his desk. He was also the foremost teaser of their new religion teacher. He was half-Swedish, had jutting ears and wanted to be addressed in the familiar *du*-form and be called brother. He was deeply religious but also a socialist and opposed to discipline. In the class, however, nobody believed in God, nobody at all liked Swedes and a socialist was something you were in Russia or if you were opposed to the military. So they teased the teacher mercilessly with his jutting ears, his Jesus, his socialism and his attempts to be familiar and brotherly with them. They teased him so much that one day he suddenly began to cry, sitting at his desk with his legs dangling feebly. His tears trickled down his cheeks and the class fell silent for a moment. He couldn't help himself. Father, father, why have you forsaken me? he whispered to the teacher who immediately jumped down from the desk and ran from the classroom. And they all roared with laughter, and he was even more a hero than he had been before.

112

Why did he remember so much precisely from that last year of intermediate school? Because it was the year his mother died? What had happened to him the year before? That was the year he was confirmed. He was given a wristwatch with luminous hands and a grey watchband and during the summer he was on a farm on Langeland where he helped out in the stables and in fencing the land. He remembered a special smell there was in the loft above the stables; a smell of hay and cow-dung and urine but also of something else he knew but couldn't place. Crab apples? Rotten pears? How do you smell a smell many years after – *without* smelling it? Smells especially kept coming to him; the smell of burlap in the basement where the scout cubs he joined for six months hung out; the smell of a particular tobacco in his father's study which gradually led him to recall how it was arranged, with the desk placed diagonally across one corner, the books to the left and the easy-chair with ear flaps at the window facing the lake with the trees on the bird island and swans landing. The smell of varnish in the school building, the fresh smell of sesame seeds outside the corner bakery, the smell of seaweed and wet wood at the public bath, and the smell of Virginia cigarettes which permeated the city during the summer of his first vacation which led him to remember everything from the trucks taking away their neighbors' furniture to the puppy he found in a stairway and brought home but wasn't allowed to keep with the result that he pulled all the bottles out of the medicine closet in his mother's bedroom in a rage and was beaten with his father's belt. Ought he to start with the smells if he wanted to recall his life down to the last details? Ought he to begin as far back as he could remember and list the first smell of his life and then add one smell after the other to it? What was the first smell of his life? The smell of his bed? Of the nurse bending over him? Of milk from his mother's breast?

After working most of the day writing down entries he was more than exhausted when he finally went to bed after frying an egg or two. Then a thousand and one new memories would appear, and sometimes he would dream his entire life, but when he awoke and turned on the light and felt for his pen and paper on the bedside table he had forgotten most of it. And gradually his memories changed. The good points turned up more and more rarely; on the other hand, he recalled every occasion on which he had done harm, had teased somebody, annoyed somebody, hit somebody. Two memories in particular returned constantly: the memory of the shoemaker's son whom he had struck with a piece of coal and the memory of the religion teacher who had fled weeping from the classroom. Sometimes he was even afraid to stir up his memories and avoided making notes – what he had was strong enough to resist the Helpers when they came to give him a new personality and another name. But it was all the worse at night. Now it wasn't smells but faces which appeared, one after the other, faces from his years at grade school and intermediate school, faces from his high school years, from his time at university, in a disconnected sequence and in all different sizes. One moment it was the face of a scout cub whose cap he had thrown in the lake, the next it was the face of a young actor he had criticized cruelly while he was substituting briefly as a theatrical critic on a morning paper. For a long time rumors circulated to the effect that he had destroyed the actor's career with that review. He saw the actor's face that morning as he opened the paper and read the review which ended with the following words about him: 'what is to be done with this colossal want of talent?' The actor read the review again, his face went chalk white, and he crumpled the paper and threw it on the floor. His face gradually became the only thing he could see in the endless dark; it appeared and disappeared. Disembodied, it circled in a strange motion and suddenly became the face of the religion teacher and soon after that the face of the shoemaker's son with tears squirting horizontally from his eyes.

His nights became a series of nightmares about faces with painful expressions, and when he awoke and turned on the light and sat up on the edge of the bed it was as though his life

114

had consisted of nothing but hurting other people. What had since happened to the religion teacher? Had he died ten years ago from a heart attack? What had happened to the shoemaker's son? Had he for ever been branded by his remark that fuel was only for those who hadn't sided with the Nazis? Had he become locked up in himself, hateful and desperate, a man beside himself, perhaps one of the patients at the state hospital who walked about with their eyes on the ground, a petrified memory of a winter's day when he had been hit on the head with a piece of coal for something he hadn't done? And the actor? Had he gone down with drink when no one would use him; was he now in an alcoholics' home, an old, bitter man? Or had he committed suicide?

He hurriedly took a pill and smoked a few cigarettes, but he couldn't free himself of the notion that he had been destined to do harm and that there was a close connection between the day he hit the shoemaker's son on the head and the night he hammered Edith's head against the wall and later the floor. Were there some people who were *born* evil? And was he one of them? He gave up writing anymore and hid all the sheets of paper in his desk drawer. He had gradually become more afraid of what it said on them and of the thousands of new faces appearing if he kept on writing than he was of the Helpers' imminent attempts to change him. But he could not exorcize the faces that had already appeared to him. They populated his apartment, hid behind the wallpaper to appear when darkness fell, crowded under his bed and his chair and his rug. They whispered to him about all the evil things he had done to them, how he had broken their lives just because he needed to show off. His terror of the faces soon grew so deep that he ran away from the apartment and wandered around among the blocks, even thinking of going to the Helpers to find out what he could do about them. But they would just send him on more hate trips with the result that even more faces would appear, faces which he would begin by exterminating, shooting and murdering with howls and yells but which would later pursue him. These faces would beg him for

115

friendliness and charity which he wouldn't be able to give because many years ago, while he was still in his mother's womb, it had been decided that he was to be evil.

One afternoon he went into the city. He had to get as far away from the apartment as possible. Perhaps a ship would take him on as a sailor. Perhaps he ought to let his beard grow, get drunk and be picked up as a bum and put in one of the old railroad cars the authorities gave to the most hopeless drunks. How could he best disappear from it all? he thought as he sat in the underground and enjoyed a momentary spell of peace. Should he pretend to be a political refugee and speak a strange language so that the alien police would put him on a plane going to Latin America, from whence he would be sent to East Europe, and from there to Africa, to live out the rest of his life without a passport in mid-air between the continents? He got out at Town Hall Square, crossed against a red light and mingled with the crowds on the sidewalk.

It was the rush hour. People were finishing their shopping, pushing each other aside when they came out of the shops, yelling curses at kids who were running between their legs and brutally tugging at their dogs' leashes when they wanted to sniff at each other. Hundreds of strange, closed faces passed him, but among them were some that reminded him of the ones in his dreams. Perhaps it was the shoemaker's son over there walking along the wall as an old, bent man, spitting on the ground, wearing a worn overcoat and staring down constantly. Perhaps it was the actor there, emerging from a newly opened clinic for the lonely and looking around with empty, fearful eyes, as though he had no notion of where to go. No, he certainly would not be able to recognize him. But the shoemaker's son then? He turned around anxiously and considered running after him and apologizing for what he had done. Perhaps all the people he had harmed in his time would appear here on the boulevard, and if he just walked up and down the street for a few hours he would meet them and contact them and be forgiven.

The bent man disappeared into the crowd, but then he saw a

slightly younger man who more likely was the shoemaker's son. He had the same red hair and freckles all over his face. It was the freckles which made him certain that it was he, and he turned around and followed him and took him by the arm.

'Do you forgive me?'

'What do you mean?' the shoemaker's son asked, looking at him with desperate eyes.

'For what I did then.'

'When?'

'Then!'

The red-haired man tore his arm away and disappeared down the street, and he stood there and felt how everybody stared at him and avoided him in a huge circle as though he were a leper. From the shop-windows people were looking out at him, and from the offices, the cafeterias. His evil was visible, in his eyes, in the shape of his mouth, in his neck and in his entire tense posture. Evil radiated from him, and presently he knew that all the faces fitted the ones in his nightmares. Suddenly the religion teacher came by and avoided him in the form of a tortured old man with strangely hanging ears. And then the grade school teacher came rolling along in a wheel-chair, looking as though she were past ninety, and struck out at him with her cane. The next moment it was the boy from Langelinie, who had become a policeman and was examining him intensely as though he were hoping for a chance to fine him for doing something wrong. They were all here, as though they had agreed mutually to meet him precisely on this day, at this time, and he quickly realized that he wouldn't be able to apologize to all of them, with the result that the feeling of guilt became an unendurable pain in his back and neck, pressing behind his ears, pounding in his temples and making thousands of tiny explosions in his brain. He almost yelled as loud as he could and felt like pushing all the people aside, overturning them and trampling on them and running to a back yard or a park where there were no people who had accounts to settle with him. But he used the last remnant of self-control he had to look straight ahead and calmly walk back

117

towards Town Hall Square.

Behind him he heard how everyone shushed, and turned around to look at his back, but when he got to Town Hall Square the silence was replaced by a low whispering. He knew what they were all whispering about. They were whispering about his latest evil deed, killing his wife in the most brutal way imaginable. Their whispering rose into the air, stole along the rooftops around Town Hall Square and made the pain in his back and neck even worse; it followed him like a river of lava or something sticky that was about to grasp his ankles and glue him fast and make him fall forward and strike his head against the tiles. But he escaped at the last instant by running across the square against a red light and hurrying into a pub and slamming the door hard behind him. He looked sideways out the door for fear that the whispering of the thousand faces would push open the door and grab him in a corner and finish him off once and for all. But fortunately the door remained closed, and he went to the bar and ordered a whiskey.

The whiskey multiplied itself and now the ones at the tables also began to whisper as well as those standing by the bar. The man from tv, one whispered. Are we all going to wind up like that? whispered another. He tried to make contact with the bartender, but he too avoided him except when he ordered another whiskey. Everything began swaying around him, pictures fell off the walls, the bar rose against him like the hinged top of a desk, and he saw no other way out except reaching for the bartender and gripping his coat lapels and telling him about all the people he had harmed in his life. He talked about the boy on Langelinie and the grade school teacher and the cub whose cap he threw in the lake and the shoemaker's son and his mother's medicine closet which he plundered because he wasn't allowed to keep a puppy and the religion teacher and the actor who had probably committed suicide. Finally he talked about Edith and the bartender listened in such a way that he thought that here was finally the person who understood him and who could forgive him. But then the bartender demanded payment for all the whiskey he had drunk, leaned

118

across the bar, grabbed him and felt in his pockets until he found a banknote.

'*That* way,' the bartender said and pointed to the door.

The first spring sunshine struck him like a blow as he staggered outside and shortly after found himself in the middle of the street where the cars honked ferociously.

'Judge me!' he yelled. '*Judge* me!'

CHAPTER TEN

He was on the bird-island, digging for worms. His mother called out to him that he could play as long as he wanted. He went on digging happily; it was a warm summer's day, and all around the bird-island were lots of dinghies with sails of all different colors. Then it suddenly became dark, it began thundering, the worms came out of the ground and started crawling all over the bird-island, falling into the water and swimming away while the dinghies sailed up on land and disappeared down the side streets off the embankment. His mother called out to him again, but now she wasn't calling out of the window of their apartment, but walking across the water. He became afraid of her and walked backwards. But she kept on coming closer and closer.

'You haven't done anything wrong, Torben,' she smiled at him.

He stopped. Then he was lifted up from behind by his father and put on his shoulders, and in that instant the dinghies came back down the side street, the worms returned to their holes, the sun came out from behind black clouds while thousands of ducks and swans glided down over the lake. In the background yellow streetcars rang their bells, and in one of them sat his grandmother looking happy. Shortly after that he awoke.

He smiled. In recent weeks he had only had good dreams. They might contain sinister bits like the worms crawling out of their holes, but.they always ended well. He looked around his new room. On his desk was a tray with tea, biscuits and jam and a piece of chocolate. The nurse had probably put it there. She must have woken him when she slammed the door behind her. He got up, went to the window and looked down over the park. In one corner the theatrical group was rehearsing. In another a poet in a cloak was making dramatic gestures. Round about on the benches were people playing chess or enjoying the first real spring sunshine with their shirts unbuttoned and their pants rolled up above their knees. The trees had almost put out their leaves and the birds were mating everywhere. It was mid-afternoon, and he felt like taking a walk in the park or sitting on one of the benches and unbuttoning his shirt. But he didn't have time. Not yet. Not for another couple of years. He had finally been found guilty of Edith's death, and had been sentenced to write four big novels about the world of beauty and joy awaiting man in a not-too-distant future when present society collapsed. As a punishment for all the evil he had done he was enjoined to write the books so beautifully and fantastically that they would raise the spirits of all their readers during the years that were left before the great change would come. He had already been to the publisher and got the deadline. The first novel was to be completed by this fall, the next one by next spring and the two last the following summer and winter. He could write them exactly as he pleased, make them short or long, introduce many or few characters – as long as he was able to keep up the readers' spirits.

He already had the four novels in his head. The first was to be about the revolt of the children. About a strange boy with supernatural gifts born to ordinary parents in an ordinary supercommunity. During the first years of his life there was nothing odd about him; he cried like all other kids when he wasn't fed on time or had peed in his pants, radiated joy when he succeeded in speaking the first words and staggered to the front door on tiny legs when the bell rang and his father came home from work. But his parents quickly noticed that he was more intelligent than other children, that he possessed unbelievable energy and only needed to sleep for a few hours. When he was about five he was intellectually as well-developed as a fifteen-year-old without seeming overgrown or awkward. There was something special about this child, the parents realized, and they agreed not to reveal it to anyone before he went to school. Here he quickly became the leader of all the children, began a revolt against teachers and psychologists. He encouraged other children all over the country to join and gradually frightened society out of its wits, not by violence, nor by old-fashioned terror or actions, but by telling stories wherever he went and having other children learn them by heart and tell them again to everyone who wanted to listen; terrible stories and good stories, stories that ended sadly and stories that ended happily, stories about beasts and stories about the secrets of the sea and distant countries. Gradually all the children in the country would be telling each other stories, and at first the grownups wouldn't listen to them, but after a while even the grownups would listen and think seriously about their own lives. Then they would see how meaningless and empty it was, and so the rest of the book would be about how everybody started breaking down all the old things and building the new, the beautiful and the fantastic.

The next novel would be about old people. About a world in a distant galaxy where people would live forever if they could only get there. One day a rocket ship would land on the planet, and the contact would be made back to old Earth. Every time a person became old he would be sent to the new planet, and suddenly he would realize that life had only begun. The idea was that human life on Earth was a sort of test (which all would pass) for everlasting life on the new planet. On the old planet people would learn from mistakes, learn to think, to control

122

fear, to be considerate of others – and when they had become wise and careful they would be sent to the new planet and start building a civilization whose beauty would surpass all the beauty that had ever been on Earth.

The third novel was still a bit hazy in his mind. But it was set on the bottom of the sea where mankind would go one day soon. Here man would be able to romp and play even better than he had ever done in his best moments on land, thanks to some small artificial gills which would be developed. New, cathedral-like cities would arise on the ocean floor, new horizons, new forms of beauty, new directions in art, religion and understanding would arise in this new Atlantis.

The last book would be about Edith. It would begin realistically. He would describe everything he knew about her, describe her from the first day he met her at a cafe in Copenhagen, of their happy stay in the south of France and up to the time she surrendered to outside pressures and he, overcome by madness, killed her. He would describe her laughter, her soft skin, her tenderness to Jasper, the fragrance of her hair, her enthusiasm for her work as a film editor, her formidable skills in cooking, making things grow and other people open up and show their best sides. He would describe her making love, sleeping with her cheek on his shoulder and waking up and stretching her beautiful body. He would describe her so intensely that she would finally become alive and step out and meet the readers and be embraced by them, and then she, along with him and all the readers, would go visit the people from the first three novels. She would take them to visit the boy with the supernatural gifts and the fantastic world he had made. And then she would take them to the world of everlasting life and to the bottom of the sea with the cathedral-like cities, and the readers would choose themselves where they would want to live. Four novels. Four novels which the whole world would read and which would end with Edith and him finding one another again, meeting in a new, violent embrace, among the stars or the beauty of the sea. And Jasper would be with them.

* * *

He had two hours of work ahead of him. Then they would ring the bell for dinner. He put blank paper to the left of the typewriter, pens, pencils and erasers to the right and put a sheet of paper in the machine. He felt his body tense with excitement as he wrote: 'Chapter One'.

He leaned back. Thought carefully. Then he looked at a photograph of Edith he had been allowed to have back. It was stuck on the wall with four thumbtacks. He could feel how she was giving him strength to start the first novel.

'We won!' he said to her.

He knew she was listening, and started to write.

There were those who didn't hear him, and they were the state hospital psychiatrists, gathered in conference. He on the other hand was not able to hear them either, as they decided that the experiment to which he had been subjected must be regarded as highly successful and that it would therefore be appropriate to apply for funds for a major expansion of Happiness Park.